The Judas Tree
&
Tenbow

The Judas Tree
&
Tenbow

MATT BRAUN

St. Martin's Paperbacks

These are works of fiction. All of the characters, organizations, and events portrayed in them are either products of the author's imagination or are used fictitiously.

Published in the United States by St. Martin's Paperbacks, an imprint of St. Martin's Publishing Group.

THE JUDAS TREE / TENBOW

The Judas Tree copyright © 1982 by Matt Braun.
Tenbow copyright © 1991 by Matt Braun.

For information address St. Martin's Publishing Group, 120 Broadway, New York, NY 10271.

www.stmartins.com

ISBN: 978-1-250-25240-1

Our books may be purchased in bulk for promotional, educational, or business use. Please contact your local bookseller or the Macmillan Corporate and Premium Sales Department at 1-800-221-7945, ext. 5442, or by e-mail at MacmillanSpecialMarkets@macmillan.com.

Printed in the United States of America

The Judas Tree St. Martin's Paperbacks edition / October 2003
Tenbow St. Martin's Paperbacks edition / January 2006

10 9 8 7 6 5 4 3 2 1

The Judas Tree

To
Ron
Marty and Marnie
Milt and Peter
A team with vision and
All Westerners at heart

Author's Note

The Judas Tree is based on a true story.

The mining camps of Montana Territory were hellholes of depravity and lawlessness. None was more infamous, or alluring, than Virginia City. There, deep in the wilderness, one of the great gold bonanzas of all time was discovered. Thousands of miners were drawn by the promise of riches; not far behind them were the scavengers of the frontier, the saloonkeepers and gamblers and whores. Yet it was the outlaws and road agents who posed the gravest threat along Alder Gulch. Human predators, they robbed and killed with a savagery unequaled in the annals of the Old West. Their reign of terror ultimately claimed the lives of more than one hundred men. Wholesale murder was the order of the day in Virginia City.

Where violence flourishes there are always men willing to take the law into their own hands. Vigilante movements were common in the Old West, and justice was seldom tempered by mercy. Such was the case in Virginia City, where unchecked lawlessness gave rise to mob rule and summary execution. Not infrequently, the leaders of vigilance groups were as ruthless and coldblooded as the outlaws they hanged.

Anyone familiar with the history of Montana Territory will recognize *The Judas Tree* as a work of fiction based on fact. Some license has been taken with events and dates, and the names of certain historical characters have been changed. Yet the truth of that long-ago time has been depicted with accuracy and realism. Documented fact rather than invention forms the cornerstone of the story.

Luke Starbuck undertakes a hazardous assignment in *The Judas Tree*. His reputation as a detective and mankiller precedes him wherever he travels on the western frontier. All his talents as an undercover operative and a master of disguise are tested to the limit in Virginia City. His mission pits him against corrupt politicians, vice lords, and a murderous gang of robbers. The ultimate challenge, however, involves a confrontation with the band of stranglers who called themselves vigilantes. His investigation brings to light the volatile world of a lawless mining camp.

The Judas Tree, in the end, depicts a tale of men brutalized by events. Luke Starbuck saw it happen very much the way it's told.

Chapter One

The trolley car stopped at Seventeenth and Larimer. Starbuck swung down, waiting for a carriage to pass. Then he crossed to the corner occupied by the Windsor Hotel. His office was on Seventeenth Street, halfway down the block. He strolled along at a leisurely pace.

Denver basked under a bright August sun. To the west, the Rockies jutted skyward, still capped with snow. The air was crystal clear and the afternoon moderately warm. Starbuck's attire was casual, suitable to the weather. He wore a light corduroy jacket, a linen shirt open at the neck, and a low-crowned Stetson. Under the jacket, snugged tight in a cross-draw holster, he carried a Colt .45 at waist level. Even in Denver, he always went armed.

The office building was directly behind the hotel, across the alley. He mounted the stairs to the second floor and proceeded along a hallway. Several years ago he had established headquarters in Denver. As his business expanded, his office had grown from a modest cubbyhole to a two-room suite. His caseload generally kept him on the move, and his visits to the office, even when he was in town, were sporadic. He

turned into a doorway marked by a simple brass plac-
ard:

LUKE STARBUCK
INVESTIGATIONS

Verna Phelps, his secretary, was seated behind a
desk in the outer room. She was a spinster, pushing
forty, and seemingly resigned to the life of an old
maid. Her hair was pulled back in a severe chignon,
and pince-nez glasses dangled from a black ribbon
around her neck. She greeted him with a perfunctory
nod.

"Good afternoon."

"Afternoon, Verna." Starbuck nailed his hat on a
halltree. "What's on for today?"

"Where shall I start?"

"That bad, huh?"

"You have a full schedule."

"Well, like they say . . . no rest for the weary."

"Humph!"

Verna clamped her pince-nez on the tip of her nose.
She took great pride in his work as a detective. She
even derived a certain vicarious satisfaction from his
notoriety as a mankiller. Yet she viewed his personal
life with prim disapproval. Between cases, he devoted
his nights to Denver's sporting district and seldom
rose from bed before noon. His general attitude was
that a man who worked hard was entitled to play hard.
The upshot was what Verna considered a mild form
of debauchery. She thought it scandalous behavior for
a man in his position.

"Perhaps a *decent* night's sleep"—Verna gave him a vinegary glance—"would leave you less weary."

Starbuck yawned. "I like the indecent kind lots better."

"No doubt!" Verna flushed and handed him a stack of papers. "Here's your correspondence and the monthly report from your banker."

"Anything else?"

"You have a two o'clock appointment with Horace Griffin of Wells Fargo."

"Since when?"

"He sent a note over this morning."

"What's it about?"

"I have no idea," Verna replied. "His note simply requested an appointment."

"Here or there?"

"Here." Verna squinted over her glasses. "I thought it safe to reply you would be available—by two o'clock."

"Ouch!" Starbuck met her frosty look with a grin. "No need to draw blood."

"I merely deliver messages, nothing more."

Starbuck laughed and moved through the door to his private office. Nothing fancy, the room contained a desk and several wooden armchairs. On the far wall was a large double-door safe where confidential records were stored. He seated himself in a swivel chair behind the desk and lit a cigarette. Then, with no great enthusiasm, he began riffling through the correspondence.

The letters were routine requests for his services. So far, 1882 had proved to be a banner year. He had played an active part in the death of Jesse James, and he'd broken a criminal conspiracy in Deadwood, Dakota Territory. The cases garnered national attention, and the resulting publicity had boosted his already formidable reputation as a private detective. The volume of mail increased accordingly, and he was now being offered work from every corner of the West. Several firms had even proposed placing him on a yearly retainer. Those letters were the first to hit the wastebasket.

One thing Starbuck prized above all else was independence. His list of clients included railroads and stagelines, mining companies and banks. Yet he was extremely choosy, and money alone was never the determining factor. He accepted an assignment principally for the challenge involved; a run-of-the-mill case was simply passed over without consideration. He could afford to pick and choose by virtue of a sizable investment portfolio. The monthly statement from his banker indicated diversity and sound judgment. He owned substantial blocks of stock in railroads and mining companies, along with municipal bonds and select parcels of real estate. His total worth was approaching three hundred thousand dollars, and dividends alone provided a comfortable income. He enjoyed his work and he took pride in his craft. But he accepted an assignment only when it intrigued him. The wastebasket was constantly full.

Today was no exception. One letter out of the entire stack was set aside for reply. Then, with that bothersome chore completed, he leaned back in the swivel chair. His mind turned to Horace Griffin and the upcoming appointment. He quickly sifted through his mental catalogue on the Wells Fargo division superintendent.

Griffin had first hired him the fall of '81. The assignment had taken him to Tombstone and pitted him against Wyatt Earp. In the course of his investigation, he had established that Earp was a coldblooded murderer and the ringleader of a gang of stage robbers. The outcome, in his view, was the one black mark on his record. Try as he might—and he'd tried very hard—he had failed to kill Earp. A slippery character, Earp had refused to fight, and therefore escaped Arizona alive. His present whereabouts was unknown, and of no interest to anyone.

Still, even though Starbuck considered the job only half done, Wells Fargo had been appreciative. After Earp's departure, stage robbery had all but ceased in the Tombstone district. Griffin had put through a request for a bonus, and the head office in San Francisco had approved it without hesitation. Since then, Wells Fargo had been instrumental in steering several clients to Starbuck's doorstep. One assignment had taken him to San Francisco itself, and another had put him on the trail of Jesse James. The cases, in both instances, were unusual and challenging. So far as Starbuck was concerned, Wells Fargo was a regular tapspring of interesting work. He liked the brand of trouble they sent his way.

Some while later, Verna ushered Horace Griffin through the door. The Wells Fargo superintendent was accompanied by two men, and they trooped into the office like a trio of gravediggers. Their expressions were curiously somber, and Starbuck sensed an undercurrent of tension. Griffin made short work of the introductions.

"Luke, I'd like you to meet Munro Salisbury and John Duggan." While a round of handshakes was under way, Griffin went on. "Mr. Salisbury is senior partner of the Gilmer and Salisbury Stage Line. Mr. Duggan is president of the Virginia City Mining Association."

"Nevada?" Starbuck inquired. "Or Montana?"

"Montana," Duggan responded with a marled stare. "So far as we're concerned, it's the *only* Virginia City!"

"I admire your civic spirit, Mr. Duggan."

At Starbuck's invitation, the men took chairs in front of the desk. He was unaccustomed to dealing with committees, and he warned himself to proceed with caution. The nature of his work, which was largely undercover, demanded the utmost secrecy. For all their sepulchral mood, the delegation before him was an unknown quantity. He nodded and smiled.

"What can I do for you gentlemen?"

Griffin took the lead. "Before we get down to cases, let me fill you in on the details. Several years ago Gilmer and Salisbury bought out Wells Fargo's interests in Montana. We have an express contract with them—primarily gold shipments—but that's it. We don't actually operate the stageline ourselves."

"Sounds like a profitable arrangement."

"It was," Griffin remarked stiffly. "Up until a year or so ago. Then the holdups started, and things have gone downhill ever since."

"Oh?" Starbuck said evenly. "How many hold-ups?"

"Three or four a month, and that's just the stage-coaches! Some miners transport their bullion themselves, and they've been hit even harder. We're talking about an epidemic, Luke. Wholesale robbery!"

"And murder," Salisbury interjected gravely. "At last count fifty-six men had been killed. Twelve were stage employees or passengers, and the rest were miners."

"I'll be damned!" Starbuck suddenly looked interested. "What about the law? Why hasn't your sheriff cracked down?"

"He has!" Salisbury said hastily. "We couldn't ask for a better sheriff than Henry Palmer. In the last year alone, he's captured eleven bandits and killed four more. I might add we tried and hanged ten of those he captured. But, as Mr. Griffin told you, it's an epidemic! No peace officer can be everywhere at once."

John Duggan cleared his throat. "Are you familiar with that part of Montana, Mr. Starbuck?"

"No," Starbuck admitted. "I've only been through there once, and that was by train."

"It's rough country," Duggan explained. "Only two roads in and out of Virginia City. One to the railroad at Dillon, and the other to Butte. All of it's mountainous and heavily wooded. Perfect for outlaws—and a nightmare for lawmen."

"Offhand"—Starbuck paused, an odd smile at the corners of his mouth—"I'd say it's a matter of the wrong people getting killed."

The words were spoken in a pleasant voice. Yet

none of the men missed the quiet deadliness underlying the statement. Starbuck stared back at them with eyes that were uncommonly blue and deceptively tranquil. He was tall and wide through the shoulders, and his features were ruggedly forceful under a thatch of sandy chestnut hair. Over one eyebrow was a jagged scar, and his nose was crooked a hair off center. He looked like a blooded veteran, cold and dangerous. His moderate tone somehow underscored the impression.

Horace Griffin thought the statement revealed much about the detective. Starbuck was as deadly as the outlaws he hunted—a mankiller—the very attribute needed if ever law was to be brought to Virginia City. At length, the Wells Fargo superintendent shifted in his chair. He looked Starbuck straight in the eye.

"We'd like to retain your services, Luke."

"Why?" Starbuck asked deliberately. "From what you say, you're up against a regular army of robbers. What makes you think I'd do any better than your sheriff?"

"The sheriff's too well known for what we have in mind." Griffin hesitated, took a deep breath, and let it out slowly. "We have reason to believe the stagecoach robbers are an organized gang."

"How so?"

"The holdups appear to be planned. We think that would require someone with inside information—a Judas."

"Any idea who's behind it?"

"None whatever." Griffin frowned, shook his head.

"But if we're right, then what we need is an under-cover operative. Someone who can get to the bottom of it—and stop it."

Starbuck understood the message. He was being asked to infiltrate the gang and dispense summary justice. The gang leader—and the Judas—were to be killed. He mulled it over a moment, intrigued primarily by one aspect. He wondered why the robbers murdered their victims so casually, and so often. Then, abruptly, he turned to Duggan.

"What's your part in all this?"

"I don't follow you."

"It's simple enough," Starbuck said bluntly. "Griffin and Salisbury want the stage holdups stopped. What're you after?"

"Law and order," Duggan informed him. "At this very moment, Virginia City is on the edge of anarchy. Too many miners have been murdered, and there's no end in sight. It has to stop!"

"What do you mean . . . anarchy?"

"Vigilantes," Duggan said grimly. "One of our local hotheads is beating the drum for a vigilance committee. Unless you put a halt to these murders, he'll get his way."

"What's his name?"

"Lott," Duggan said with a grimace. "Wilbur X. Lott. He's politically ambitious, and he's using the vigilante issue as a soapbox. People are starting to listen—and that's dangerous."

Starbuck fixed him with a speculative gaze. "Do you think there's some connection between the stage robbers and whoever's robbing the miners?"

"God, I hope so!" Duggan said vehemently. "If there's not, then there's no stopping the vigilante movement!"

Starbuck was thoughtful for a time. His expression was abstracted, and he appeared to be debating something within himself. Then, at last, he looked at Griffin.

"Does anyone know you've approached me? Any of your associates, the sheriff, anyone at all?"

"No one," Griffin assured him. "These gentlemen arrived in Denver only last night. They asked my advice, and I recommended you as the man for the job. That's as far as it's gone."

Starbuck regarded him with great calmness. "I'll take the assignment on two conditions. First—I do it my own way, no questions asked. Second—all three of you button your lip till the job's done. Anybody talks out of school and I'll know where to look."

Duggan stiffened. "That sounds like a threat!"

"Take it any way you want," Starbuck said flatly. "It's good advice . . . the best you'll ever get."

"Indeed it is," Griffin broke in smoothly. "Now, what about your fee, Luke?"

"Same as last time," Starbuck said without inflection. "Five thousand down and five thousand on delivery."

"One question, Mr. Starbuck." Salisbury cocked his head with a quizzical look. "How will we contact you, once you've undertaken the job?"

"You won't." Starbuck's eyes were hard, impersonal. "You'll get a report when the assignment's completed, not before. That's the way I work."

Griffin smiled and rose to his feet. "We'll wait to hear from you, Luke."

"Depend on it, Horace."

When they were gone, Starbuck walked directly to the safe. He spun the combination knob and swung open one of the doors. On an inside shelf were four leather-bound ledgers. He took out the ledger stenciled *G-L* and returned to his desk. After lighting a cigarette, he opened the ledger to the section flagged with the letter *L*. He began thumbing through the pages.

The ledgers were a rogues' gallery of western outlaws. Almost a year ago, he'd begun collecting information on the Who's Who of the criminal element. Correspondence with peace officers and U.S. marshals across the frontier provided him with hard intelligence. Added to newspaper clippings and material gleaned from wanted dodgers, it gave him a quick and ready reference whenever he undertook a new case. He now had dossiers on more than three hundred gunmen and desperados.

A few moments later he stubbed out his cigarette. There was no page on Wilbur X. Lott, the aspiring vigilante leader. Nor was there any cross-reference indicating an alias. He'd thought it a long shot, but nonetheless worth a try. All things considered, though, it was no great loss. He was accustomed to working in the blind.

Lost in thought, he replaced the ledger and locked the safe. Then he wandered into the outer office. Verna looked up, and he stopped beside her desk.

"I took the assignment."

"So I heard."

"Eavesdropper." Starbuck smiled, nodding absently. "Check out the train schedule. I want to connect with the stageline at Dillon. That's somewhere in western Montana."

"When will you leave?"

"Couple of days ought to be soon enough."

"I'll see to it right away."

"Good." Starbuck turned toward the door. "Guess I'll call it a day. All that paperwork tuckered me out."

Verna sniffed. "Don't forget your theater tickets. A messenger brought them from Mr. Rothacker while you were in conference."

"Hell's bells!" Starbuck grumbled. "I forgot all about that!"

"No doubt you wanted to forget."

Verna extended an envelope, and he stared at it a moment. Orville Rothacker, publisher of the morning *Tribune,* was one of his few friends in Denver's society circles. He had accepted the invitation more than a week ago, and there was no way out of it now. With some reluctance, he took the envelope. There were two tickets inside.

"Who's playing, anyway?" He suddenly remembered, and frowned. "It's whatzizname—the Irish poet?"

"Oscar Wilde," Verna said sharply. "And it's neither a play nor poetry! Mr. Wilde will deliver a lecture on interior house decoration."

"No kidding?" Starbuck watched her with an indulgent smile. "A poet and a house decorator! What's he do for an encore?"

"Really!" Verna said with feisty outrage. "Some people consider Oscar Wilde a genius. You might very well be surprised!"

"Nothing surprises me." Starbuck's features mirrored cynical amusement. "Course, lots of things surprise Lola. She'll probably enjoy it."

"You're taking *her?*" Verna asked querulously. "To see Oscar Wilde?"

"What the hell!" Starbuck gave her a satiric look. "They're both in the show business . . . her and Oscar."

Verna appeared mortified. She merely stared as he chuckled and walked out the door. Her mind was reeling with the thought of him and his hussy—at the Tabor Grand Opera House!

She suddenly felt faint.

Chapter Two

Lola Montana was a vision of loveliness. She wore an exquisite gown of teal blue and a pearl choker with a sapphire in the center. The bodice of the gown was cut low and cinched at the waist, displaying her sumptuous figure to full advantage. Her flaxen hair was upswept and drawn back, with a soft cluster of curls fluffed high on her forehead. She looked at once regal and sensual.

Holding her arm, Starbuck was attired in a cutaway coat and black tie. Orville Rothacker and his wife, directly ahead of them, were following an usher down the aisle. The opera house was packed to capacity, and their entrance caused a sudden stir of commotion. Heads craned and the audience buzzed, all eyes turned in their direction. Starbuck was amused by the reaction, his face fixed in a nutcracker grin. He looked proud as punch.

Certain conventions were normally observed at the Tabor Grand Opera House. The boxes and all of the orchestra were reserved for the elite of Denver society. The sporting crowd and other assorted riffraff were consigned to the upper balcony. Tonight, for the first time in memory, the customary order of things had been breached. Yet no one in the audience raised a cry, and none would dare reproach Orville Rothacker. The publisher knew where all the skeletons were buried, and the lorgnette set of Capitol Hill lived in fear he would unearth the darker secrets of their past. Scandal, despite Denver's cosmopolitan airs, was still very much in vogue.

In truth, Rothacker cared nothing for their conventions or their secrets. He considered himself a newspaperman, and his friendship with Starbuck stemmed from a series of interviews over the past several years. He'd always found the detective forthcoming, however sensational the case, and the interviews never failed to boost circulation. Only on one subject had they come to an impasse. Starbuck either deflected or ignored any question as to the number of men he'd killed. Rothacker privately speculated that the number was twenty or more, perhaps many more. He hoped one day to print the full story, for he believed Starbuck deserved all the credit normally accorded sworn lawmen. Tonight, however, there was no thought of a story. He was content to enjoy the manhunter's company.

The houselights dimmed as the usher seated them. Lola squeezed Starbuck's arm and snuggled closer. She was a tawny blond cat of a girl, with bold eyes and enchanting verve. Her evenings were usually spent prancing about the stage of the Alcazar Variety Theater. The star of the show, she belted out songs in a husky alto and bewitched the crowd with her sultry good looks. The combination had made her the toast of Denver's Tenderloin district, and every man's fantasy. Yet she was one man's woman, and never prouder of it than now. Tonight he'd flaunted her before the society swells, which amounted to a public announcement. She was Luke Starbuck's woman. His only woman.

The curtain rose to reveal a lectern positioned stage center. Then a spotlight flared and Oscar Wilde walked from the wings. He was a short, plump man, with cherubic features and curly locks that tumbled to his shoulders. He wore a purple velvet coat, knee breeches, and silk stockings. In his right hand he carried a single lily, which somehow compounded the effect of his costume. He stopped behind the lectern, gazing raptly a moment at the lily, and finally looked up. The audience twittered with laughter and gave him a modest round of applause.

"Just between us, lover," Lola whispered in Starbuck's ear, "he ought to trade that lily for a pansy."

"You think so?"

"I'll lay odds he's queer as a three-dollar bill!"

"No bet!" Starbuck chortled. "I got a hunch I'd lose."

Billed as the Apostle of Aestheticism, Wilde was currently in the midst of a grand tour of America. His career as a poet-playwright had already brought him much fame in Ireland and England, and he'd been treated as a dignitary by the eastern press. In one interview, he had stated that the purpose of his tour was to bring culture to the "colonists." Tonight his reception was something less than overwhelming. Westerners apparently weren't ready for culture or the finer points of aesthetic expression. His lecture on interior decorating played to stifled yawns and impromptu bursts of laughter. Even the *grandes dames* of Denver society were hard pressed to stay awake. He cut the lecture short and marched offstage in a towering snit. The performance drew scattered applause, and a rush for the doors.

Starbuck and Lola traded smiles and said nothing. Stepping aside, they waited while Rothacker and his wife made their way to the aisle. Rothacker's mutton-chop whiskers were split wide in a wry grin. He motioned toward the stage.

"Would you like to meet the illustrious Mr. Wilde?"

"Who?" Starbuck croaked dumbly. "Me?"

"Why not?" Rothacker laughed. "We plan to interview him tomorrow, before his second lecture. That should be good for an introduction."

"I—"

"We'd love it!" Lola interrupted with a mischievous smile. "Wouldn't we, Luke?"

Starbuck gave her a hard look. "You really want to?"

"Ooo pleeze!" Her eyes sparkled with suppressed mirth. "Just for me!"

"Well—"

"It's settled, then," Rothacker said quickly. "Come along, Luke! A little culture never hurt anybody."

The publisher led the way backstage. The door to Wilde's dressing room was open, and four women, gushing compliments, were just leaving. The poet looked a little frazzled and somewhat sour around the mouth. His smile was forced.

Rothacker simply walked in and began talking. A seasoned newshound, he employed flattery with the subtle touch of a diplomat. Wilde, who was a creature of his own vanity, responded immediately. By the time introductions were completed, he was once more in character, pompous and wholly self-centered. Yet he seemed taken with Starbuck. There was a twinkle in his eye, and, to Lola's delight, he ignored everyone else. He put a chubby finger to his lips, contemplative.

"Starbuck." He repeated the name slowly. "Ah, but of course! You're the detective fellow, aren't you?"

Starbuck looked uncomfortable. "How'd you know that?"

"Why, dear man!" Wilde trilled breezily. "I read about you while I was in New York. One of those publications peculiar to America. The *Police Gazette*, I believe it was called. But a splendid article nonetheless! Indeed it was."

Starbuck smiled without warmth. "I guess I missed that issue."

"Then more's the pity!" Wilde said cheerily. "A truly gripping account it was! All about that poor sod you laid to rest in Deadwood."

A pained expression came over Starbuck's face. "I wouldn't exactly call him a poor sod."

"Well, no matter!" Wilde laughed, and his voice went up a couple of octaves. "You put the bugger out of his misery! And didn't I say to myself what a grand name for it? Deadwood! So apropos, and imagery at its purest. Now, don't you agree?"

Starbuck stifled the impulse to say what he was really thinking. "I'll take your word for it."

"Pathos, dear fellow!" Wilde made an effeminate gesture and laid his hand on Starbuck's arm. "Poets love tragedy, and a tragic figure even more. We're all very sensitive, you know?"

Lola smiled and took a possessive grip on Starbuck's other arm. "I've told Luke that very thing, Mr. Wilde! You see, I'm an artiste myself . . . a singer."

"How nice." Wilde gave her a withering look, then turned swiftly to Rothacker. "Now, about the interview you requested. I regret to say a second lecture in Denver appears fruitless. I've an engagement in Leadville, and I believe I'll travel there tomorrow."

"That's a shame," Rothacker said affably. "You might have drawn a better audience tomorrow night."

"I think not." Wilde shook his head with a condescending air. "Aestheticism does require a certain sophistication."

Rothacker grunted, smothering a laugh. "I wish you luck, then. Leadville's one of our rougher mining camps."

"Indeed!" Wilde arched one eyebrow and looked down his nose. "Well, now, I've great rapport with the working class. I wouldn't wonder they'll embrace the message with open arms!"

The conversation ended there. Wilde saw them to the door and closed it firmly. Outside, Rothacker pantomimed a limp-wristed gesture and rolled his eyes at Starbuck. Waving him off, Starbuck lagged back and took Lola by the elbow. His voice was sardonic.

"You've got some sense of humor."

Lola mimicked his dour expression. "Whatever do you mean?"

"Don't play coy!" Starbuck muttered. "You jumped at the chance to get me and Wilde together. You all but sicced the bastard on me!"

"Why, Luke Starbuck!" Lola batted her china-blue eyes. "Would I do a thing like that?"

"You not only would—you did!"

"Honestly, lover!" Her eyes seemed to glint with secret amusement. "I saved you from a fate worse than death! Your face went white when he latched on to your arm."

Starbuck's mouth suddenly split in a lopsided grin. "One thing's for sure! That little sweet pea probably won't make it out of Leadville alive. They'll stick his aesthetics where the sun don't shine!"

Lola's throaty laughter floated out over the opera house. A few moments later, on the street, Starbuck declined Rothacker's invitation to a late supper. Then he flagged a hansom cab and assisted Lola inside. They drove straight to the Brown Palace Hotel, where he'd maintained a suite for the past several years. Only recently had Lola become a permanent fixture in his life and the sole partner in his bed. He took her there now, and neither of them spoke a word. Their sense of urgency was mutual, somehow heightened by the evening.

Within minutes, naked and disheveled, they were locked together.

Starbuck kissed the vee between her breasts. Then he rolled away and sprawled exhausted on the bed. She wiggled into the crook of his arm and pillowed her head on his shoulder. For a while, time lost measure and meaning. She lay still and sated, far beyond the limits of her most vivid fantasies. She felt fulfilled and wanted.

Yet deep within she knew she possessed only a part of him. She was his woman, but he was still his own man. He shared his secrets with her and confided in her as he would in no other human. There was implicit trust in that sharing, for at root he was a man of privacy and ingrained cynicism. She accepted those things, careful never to smother him or demand more than he could give. She understood him with a wisdom that was both intuitive and practical. Only by allowing him to go free was she assured he would return. She was content with the arrangement, secure in the knowledge that he needed her. He would never give all of himself, but the bond between them was the single bond in his life. She asked no more.

Presently Starbuck stirred. He pulled her close and held her quietly for a moment. Then he nuzzled her unbound hair, his voice muted and curiously gentle.

"I leave day after tomorrow."

"You—you've taken another case?"

Starbuck bobbed his head. "Wells Fargo and another stageline hired me. They've got a little problem with a gang of robbers. Nothing too serious."

"I'll bet!" She tweaked the hair on his chest. "You're not fooling anybody, lover-man. If it wasn't serious, they wouldn't come to you!"

"All in a day's work," Starbuck said easily. "Wouldn't be any fun if it wasn't sticky."

"Where are they sending you?"

"Virginia City," Starbuck told her. "The one in Montana."

Lola sat bolt upright. Her breasts shimmered in the glow of lamplight spilling through the parlor door. She stared down at him with an expression of mild wonder.

"I was offered a job in Virginia City!"

"Yeah?" Starbuck asked idly. "Who by?"

Her brow furrowed in concentration. "Stinson? No, wait a minute. It was Stimson. Omar Stimson! He owns the Gem Theater there."

"How come he contacted you?"

"Thanks a lot!" Lola gave him a pouty look. "Whether you know it or not, I've made a name for myself, too. All kinds of people have tried to hire me away from Jack Brady! It just so happens I like the Alcazar and I like Denver."

Starbuck chuckled softly. "I guess folks know a good thing when they see it."

"They certainly do!" She tossed her head. "Stimson offered me a thousand dollars for *one week* in Virginia City!"

"Jesus!" Starbuck was impressed. "He must've meant business!"

"Of course he did," Lola replied airily. "In case you haven't noticed, I do tend to draw a crowd."

"You've got a way with men, all right. I reckon I'd be the first to admit it."

Lola fell silent a moment. A strange look came over her face, and she seemed to stare straight through him. Then she suddenly giggled and squirmed around like soft wax.

"Holy Hannah!" she squealed. "I just had a brain-storm!"

"Since you're gonna tell me anyway, go ahead."

"Just suppose—" She hesitated, her eyes bright as berries. "Now, hear me out before you say any-thing. Just suppose I took the job in Virginia City. I could—"

"No!" Starbuck cut her short. "Thumbs down, and that's final!"

"Just listen, for God's sake!" She scooted closer and went on in a rush. "I could be your ears and your eyes. You'd be amazed what a girl picks up around men! Not to mention what I could worm out of Stim-son himself. He probably knows everybody who's anybody in Virginia City!"

"I said no, and that's that."

"Aww c'mon, lover!" she cooed. "How many chances will we have to work together? It's made to order, once in a lifetime!"

"You're wasting your breath," Starbuck said ston-ily. "I don't need any help, and on top of that, it's too dangerous. The people I'm after are cutthroats and murderers! One slip and you'd wind up with your neck on the chopping block."

"Oh, don't be silly!" she said, lifting her chin. "I've been twisting men around my little finger all my life. Do you really think I couldn't do it in Virginia City? Do you?"

"I didn't say that," Starbuck mumbled. "I just said it's too dangerous."

"Have a heart, Luke." Her voice dropped to a whisper. "I want to do it. And I'd be good at it! You know I would."

"I still say no," Starbuck murmured uneasily. "Besides, you can't quit your job at the Alcazar. There's no sense to it."

"Forget Jack Brady!" she hooted. "If I want a week off, he'll grin and bear it. Believe me, he will! He wouldn't *dare* risk losing me to another joint in Denver."

Starbuck was tempted. Her logic was indisputable, and the danger was far less than he'd claimed. No one would suspect a famous variety star of being an undercover operative. There was, moreover, the lack of hard intelligence about the gang. An extra set of eyes and ears would be a tremendous asset in Virginia City. At length, still not fully convinced, he took a deep breath and exhaled slowly. His tone was tentative.

"I'll think about it."

"Hotdamn!" She laughed and clapped her hands like an exuberant child. "I'll wire Stimson first thing in the morning."

"Hold your horses!" Starbuck barked gruffly. "I said I'll *think* about it. That's all, nothing more!"

"Anything you say, lover."

Lola let it drop there. He held out his arms, and she lowered herself into his embrace. She nestled close against him, warm and cuddly and submissive. Yet her eyes danced merrily, and inside she was jubilant.

She knew she had won.

· · ·

Late the next afternoon Starbuck and Lola entered a
shop on Blake Street. He still had grave misgivings
about their plan, and his mood was somber. But she'd
cajoled and wheedled, and an hour ago the last obsta-
cle had been removed. Omar Stimson, owner of the
Gem Theater, had replied to her wire. She was booked
for a one-week engagement in Virginia City.

Inside the shop, they were greeted by Daniel Cameron. He was a master gunsmith and Starbuck's personal armorer. Unknown to anyone but themselves,
he had developed an advanced .45 cartridge that was
a deadly manstopper. He advised Starbuck on weapon
selection and kept the detective's guns in superb
working order. Wizened and gray-haired, he was considered the dean of western gunsmiths.

Starbuck trusted no man completely. A careless
word, however inadvertent, might very well jeopard-
ize the assignment. So he told Cameron only the salient details, omitting any mention of Virginia City.
Cameron was momentarily stunned by what he heard.
He knew the manhunter to be a loner; the idea of an
assistant seemed somehow foreign. All the more so
since the assistant was a woman, and one greatly ad-
mired by Cameron. He glanced at Lola a couple of
times but kept his own qualms about the arrangement
to himself. When Starbuck finished talking, Cameron
nodded sagely and spread his hands on the showcase
counter.

"How can I help you, Luke?"

"She'll need a gun," Starbuck said quietly. "A hideout of some sort, just in case she gets in a tight fix."

Cameron sometimes joined them for a drink at the Alcazar. He was on a first-name basis with the girl, and he turned to her now with a frank stare. "The truth, Lola. How familiar are you with firearms?"

"No big mystery!" Lola cocked her thumb and forefinger. "All you do is point and pull the trigger!"

"In other words," Starbuck said in a resigned voice, "she doesn't know beans. So the simpler the better— something foolproof!"

"A tall order," Cameron observed. "But if we're talking about a tight fix, then it would probably be at point-blank range."

Opening the showcase, he took out a Colt New Line Pocket Revolver. Some six inches long, it was single-action, chambered for .41 caliber, and held five rounds. He laid the Colt on the counter and next brought out an over/under-barreled Remington Derringer. A stubby weapon, roughly half the size of the Colt, the derringer was .41 caliber and held two shots. He tapped one, then the other, with his finger.

"Both are effective at close range," he noted. "The Colt has the advantage of five shots. Otherwise, there's little to choose between."

"You forgot something, Daniel." Starbuck looked Lola up and down. "Her stage clothes don't leave much room for concealment. Leastways, they don't conceal a helluva lot of *her.*"

"Very funny!" Lola gave him a sassy grin. "I don't recall any complaints before!"

"No, Luke's right," Cameron agreed. "The Colt

would never do. It's much too large, and your costumes are much too . . . revealing."

Starbuck inspected her with a clinical eye. "How about that garter you always wear? The big wide one, just above your knee. Any chance you could pull it up higher?"

"How high?"

"High enough so it wouldn't show when you flash your legs."

"I don't see why not."

"Here." Starbuck handed her the derringer. "Stick that in your garter, and you're all set. It goes where you go, and nobody the wiser."

Lola hefted the stubby pistol. "I only see one problem."

"What's that?"

"Hidden way up *there*"—a devilish smile played at the corners of her mouth—"it'll sure slow down my draw!"

"Well, if it comes down to it," Starbuck deadpanned, "you could always fake 'em out. Nobody'd expect you to show 'em a gun—up there."

Lola blushed, and Cameron suppressed a laugh. Then, still chuckling to himself, Starbuck took the derringer and demonstrated how it worked. Thumbing the tiny hammer back, he pressed the trigger; repeating the process emptied both barrels in quick succession. He next explained the loading mechanism and the method of gingerly lowering the hammer once the gun was loaded. Lola got the knack of it in short order and was soon handling the derringer with practiced ease. Satisfied, Starbuck finally allowed her to load it and stuff it into her purse. Cameron threw in a box of shells on the deal, and after Starbuck paid him, he walked them to the door. There the two men shook hands and Lola gave the gunsmith a peck on the cheek.

Outside, arm in arm, Starbuck and the girl strolled off toward the center of town. Cameron paused in the doorway, watching until they rounded the corner. He had no idea where they were headed or what their assignment entailed. Nor was he interested in learning the particulars. Certain things about the manhunter were best left unknown. Yet one thing was uppermost in his mind. A new thought that brought with it a sly, wrinkled grin.

Starbuck and Lola Montana made the perfect team. A mix of nerve and spunk, with an added dash of deadliness. A tough act.

Chapter Three

Starbuck crossed into Montana a week later. From Denver to Salt Lake City, he had taken an overnight train. There he'd switched to the narrow-gauge Utah Northern, which was the only line north through the mountains. He was traveling in disguise, and his cover name was Lee Hall.

The Utah Northern crossed the Continental Divide at Monida Pass. The elevation was almost seven thousand feet, and the tracks then dropped sharply into the Beaverhead Valley of Montana. West of the valley, the Bitterroot Range rose majestically into the clouds. To the east, the battlements of the Rocky Mountains towered skyward. The terrain was rugged, with thick pine forests and sheer canyons, all interlaced with a dizzying network of streams and rivers. It was a land of bitter winters and short summers, at once inhospitable and alluring. Yet no man went there without feeling the pull of something elemental. A sense of having stepped backward in time.

The town of Dillon was a mountain way station. Crude and windswept, it consisted primarily of warehouses and freight outfits. There the goods and supplies hauled in by the railroad were off-loaded;

lumbering Studebaker wagons then completed delivery to the mining camps and settlements of southwestern Montana. For those traveling to the hinterlands, Dillon was also the rail terminus. While the Utah Northern continued on to Butte, outlying areas were accessible only by stagecoach. The Gilmer & Salisbury line was the principal carrier.

The train arrived in Dillon shortly before noon. Starbuck stepped down from the lead coach, carrying a battered warbag. He wore rough clothing—woolen jacket and linsey shirt—and his pants were stuffed into mule-eared boots. His face was covered with whiskery stubble, and he smelled as rank as a billy goat. A handlebar mustache, one of many theatrical props he employed, was glued to his upper lip with spirit gum. His overall appearance was that of a toughnut, someone who managed a livelihood without actually working. He might have been a grifter or a thimblerigger or a robber. He looked vaguely predatory and dangerous.

Operating undercover demanded a certain gift for subterfuge. Early on in his career, Starbuck had discovered in himself something of the actor. That trait, combined with a flair for disguise, allowed him to assume a variety of roles. Over the years, his ability to transform himself into someone else had played a vital part in his survival. Articles in national publications—which invariably carried his photo—had robbed him of anonymity. His face was known and his reputation as a mankiller was widely circulated. So the characters he portrayed were crafted with an eye to outward appearance. Then he worked out a cover story, added a few quirks and mannerisms, and Luke Starbuck simply ceased to exist. His life rested solely on the skill of his performance.

Walking away from the train depot, his thoughts centered on guile and subterfuge. Lola had preceded him to Virginia City by one day. She would be playing herself, the visiting celebrity and headliner at the Gem Theater. Yet a worm of doubt still gnawed at him regarding her performance offstage. How well she handled herself, and how subtly she asked questions, would prove the critical factors. Then, too, her manner toward him would require a performance in itself. He'd told her that he would make the initial contact; whether openly or in secret would depend on the situation. For all his coaching, she was nonetheless a tyro, inexperienced at undercover work. A smile, even a familiar look, might easily tip their game. There was no margin for error, and no second chance in the event something went wrong. He worried about that a lot.

The noon stage was about to depart when he arrived at the station. He purchased a ticket, casually inquiring about the route. The agent informed him Virginia City was some thirty miles east of Dillon and there was one stop along the way. Barring the unforeseen, the stage would pull into Virginia City before sundown. Outside again, he tossed his warbag to the driver and climbed aboard the coach. Then he pulled his hat down over his eyes and settled back in the seat.

His thoughts immediately returned to Lola.

• • •

Alder Gulch wound through hillsides choked with pine and quaking aspen. Daylight Creek coursed down the gulch in an easterly direction and eventually emptied into the Madison River. A short distance up the gulch lay one of the great gold bonanzas of the western frontier. It was called Virginia City.

Wallace Street, the town's central thoroughfare, was a seething anthill. Some fifteen thousand men were working claims along the gulch, and more were arriving daily. Knots of miners crowded every corner, and the boardwalks were a shoulder-to-shoulder jostling match. The general hubbub of shouts and drunken laughter was deafening and constant. Above it all rose the strident chords of rinky-dink pianos mixed with the wail of fiddles and the sprightly twang of banjos. The rowdy throngs and the discordant sounds were somehow reminiscent of a circus gone wild.

The street itself was little more than a hurdy-gurdy collection of saloons, gambling dives, and dance halls. There were hotels and cafés, along with a couple of banks and an assortment of business establishments. But the town's commerce was devoted largely to separating the miners from their gold dust. Sin was for sale, and every joint, from the rawest busthead saloon to the dollar-a-dance palace, had a bevy of rouge-cheeked charmers. The girls were decked out in spangles and short skirts, and their faces were painted brighter than a carnival Kewpie doll. Their one mission in life was to beguile the customers with sweet talk and snakehead whiskey. Anything extra was negotiable.

Darkness had fallen over Virginia City when Starbuck pushed through the doors of the Gem Theater. The crowd inside was a mixed bag, mainly teamsters and miners. Men were standing three deep at the bar, and every table in the place was occupied. The gambling layouts—everything from faro to chuck-a-luck—were ranged along the wall opposite the bar. Toward the rear of the room there was a small orchestra pit, directly below the footlights of a wide stage. No musicians were in sight, and the stage curtain was drawn.

Starbuck shouldered through the mob at the bar. He ordered whiskey and paid the barkeep. Then he turned one elbow hooked over the counter, and inspected the room. The evening had only begun, and he assumed it was still too early for the night's opening stage show. Yet the place was already jammed, with more men crowding through the door every minute. All the signs indicated that Lola Montana would be playing to standing room only. In the meantime, while the men waited for the show, there was no scarcity of entertainment. An ivory-tickler was pounding an upright piano near the end of the bar. A small dance floor was packed with miners and house girls, whooping and stomping in a wild swirl. It looked curiously like a wrestling match set to music.

Looking past the dancers, Starbuck suddenly spotted Lola. She was seated at a table down front, close to the orchestra pit. Beside her was a barrel-gutted giant of a man. He was wide and tall, and despite his girth he appeared solid as a rock. His face was pitted with deep pockmarks, and he had flat, muddy eyes. He was talking with expansive gestures and staring at Lola with a wolfish smile. On the table was an ice bucket and a bottle of champagne, and their glasses were full. The man paused to quaff a drink, then went on talking. Lola merely sipped, listening attentively.

On impulse, Starbuck decided to take a chance. His plan, loosely formulated, was to establish himself as a hardcase and somehow infiltrate the gang of stage-coach robbers. Before then, however, he needed to make contact with Lola and determine what she'd learned thus far. But it had to be done without arousing suspicion, and the moment at hand appeared made to order. He thought he might easily bring down two birds with one stone.

Starbuck chugged his whiskey and placed the glass on the bar. Then he walked straight to the table where Lola and the man were seated. She looked up, genuinely surprised and somewhat startled. Still, she kept her wits, and no sign of recognition passed between them. Starbuck ignored the man.

"How about it, little lady?" He grinned broadly. "Wanna take a twirl around the dance floor?"

"Shove off!" the man rumbled. "Miss Montana don't dance with strangers."

"Lee Hall's the name." Starbuck's grin widened to a smirk. "I take it you're Mister Montana?"

"You take it wrong!" The man glowered at him through slitted eyes. "The name's Pete Johnson, and you'd better mark it down. Around here, I'm better know as bull o' the woods."

"Well, don't that take the cake!" Starbuck laughed,

spread his hands. "Folks generally allow I'm cock of the walk."

"Lemme tell you something, sonny." Johnson hitched his chair back and stood. He jabbed Starbuck in the chest with a thorny finger. "Close your flytrap and make tracks, or I'm gonna stunt your growth!"

Starbuck hit him without warning. Johnson went down like a poled ox, blood seeping out of his mouth. Yet he was clearly a scrapper of some experience, and uncommonly agile for all his bulk. He rolled away, scattering tables and chairs as he came to his feet. Then he advanced on Starbuck, snarling a murderous oath.

Coldly, with the look of a man who was enjoying himself, Starbuck waited. Johnson launched a haymaker, and he easily slipped inside the blow. Shifting slightly, his shoulder dipped and he sank his fist in the big man's underbelly. A whoosh of air burst out of Johnson, and he doubled over, clutching himself with a breathless woofing sound. Starbuck exploded two splintering punches on his chin.

Johnson reeled backward into the orchestra pit and sat down heavily. He shook his head, groggy from the punishment he'd absorbed but not yet done for. He planted one arm on the floor and started to lever himself upright. Starbuck took a couple of steps forward and methodically kicked him in the head. The impact collapsed him, and his skull bounced off the floor like a ripe melon. Then a shudder swept through his massive frame and he settled onto his back. He was out cold.

Starbuck dusted his hands and turned toward the

table. He saw three housemen headed in his direction, all of them carrying bungstarters. Lola idly waved them off and beckoned to him. A nervous ripple of laughter went through the crowd as the bruisers veered around him and approached the orchestra pit. He waited until they'd dragged Johnson away, then walked to the table. He doffed his hat in an elaborate bow.

"Little lady," he said in a loud, cheery voice, "I shorely hope I haven't caused you any trouble."

"Perish the thought!" Lola graced him with a dazzling smile. "Would you care for a glass of champagne, Mr. Hall?"

"Why, thank you, ma'am!" Starbuck seated himself and tilted his hat at a rakish angle. "Don't mind if I do."

"To the victor!" Lola lifted her glass in a toast. "A man as good as his brag—cock of the walk!"

Starbuck let go a great bellywhopper of a laugh. He filled Johnson's empty glass and drank to her toast. The crowd slowly lost interest, and people at nearby tables went back to their own affairs. The ivory-tickler struck up a lively tune and the wrestling match on the dance floor once more resumed. Lola leaned forward, still smiling a devastating smile. Her voice was low and conspiratorial.

"That was some entrance you made, lover!"

"Worked out pretty good." Starbuck sipped champagne, watching her over the rim of his glass. "Got us together and let everybody know Lee Hall's in town. You just keep acting like I've charmed you out of your drawers. That way we can have a drink every night and swap information."

"No problem," Lola said brightly. "The joker you whipped really was bull o' the woods! Nobody will come anywhere near me—not when you're around."

"What's the story on Johnson?"

"I know everyone is scared witless of him! Even Stimson—the owner of this joint—caters to him. He asked me as a special favor to have a drink with the big gorilla. We were just getting acquainted when you showed up."

"How're things otherwise?"

"Christ!" Lola spat in a sibilant tone. "It's no wonder Stimson offered me a thousand a week. To put it charitably, the boys in Virginia City are a little uncouth. You ought to hear what they shout when I'm onstage!"

Starbuck smiled. "Never saw a miner yet with any class. Course, as I recall, you asked to come here. Nobody twisted your arm."

"You're all heart!" Lola said sweetly. "Maybe I shouldn't tell you what I've learned by keeping my eyes open!"

"No more wisecracks," Starbuck promised. "What'd you find out?"

"Well, for one thing," Lola said in a hushed voice, "there's something funny about Stimson. I noticed it today, when I was rehearsing with the band. He's got an office upstairs, and there was a regular parade through there all afternoon." She paused, toying with her champagne glass. "From the looks of them, they're all part of the sporting crowd. I've been around enough to recognize the type."

Starbuck was thoughtful a moment. "Hard to say what it means. Offhand, though, I'd doubt it has anything to do with the gang."

"That's the other thing!" Lola's eyes got big and round. "So far as I can tell—there's no gang!"

"No gang?" Starbuck looked at her seriously. "How'd you come by that?"

"I got the musicians talking. We were taking a break, and I just casually mentioned I'd heard about the stagecoach robbers. Told them I was scared to death the whole trip over here from Dillon."

"What was their reaction?"

"Oh, the robbers are real enough! Nobody denies that. But everyone believes it's several gangs, all operating on their own. Not a single word—not even a rumor—about *one* gang leader!"

"I hope to hell they're wrong," Starbuck said, troubled. "Otherwise we're here on a wild-goose chase."

"Speak of the devil!"

Starbuck glanced around and saw the musicians drifting into the orchestra pit. He turned back to Lola. "Time for the first show?"

"Almost." She pulled a face. "Will you wait till I'm through?"

"Not tonight. We don't want to give anyone ideas."

"I'm staying at the Virginia Hotel—room two-oh-four—in case you get any ideas."

"We'll see," Starbuck said evasively. "However it works out, let me contact you. Don't make any moves on your own."

"Anything you say, lover." Lola rose and gave him a brilliant smile. Her voice was gay and pitched loud enough to be heard over the drone from nearby tables. "I do want to thank you for a lovely conversation, Mr. Hall. Drop around anytime! You're always welcome."

"I shorely will, Miss Montana! That's a puredee promise!"

Lola nodded and walked toward a door leading backstage. Starbuck lit a cigarette and poured himself another glass of champagne. He decided to stay for the show and then move on to another joint. While he hadn't mentioned it, he was registered at the Virginia Hotel, and he thought he might look in on her later. He was abruptly jerked back to the present when a man halted beside the table.

"Evening."

"Hullo." Starbuck looked at him through a wreath of smoke. "Help you with something?"

"I'd like to talk with you a minute. Mind if I have a chair?"

"All depends on who's asking."

"Omar Stimson. I own the place."

Starbuck shrugged and waved his hand. "Take a load off your feet."

"Thanks."

Stimson was short and heavyset, paunchy around the middle. His face was moonlike and his nose was veined red from an intimate acquaintance with liquor. A long black cigar jutted from his mouth. He lowered himself into a chair.

"You're pretty handy with your fists."

"I get by," Starbuck allowed. "That fellow a friend of yours?"

"Johnson?" Stimson shook his head. "No, he's just one of the regulars. Asked me to introduce him to Miss Montana, and I did the honors."

"Way he acted, anybody would've thought he had a bill of sale on the lady."

"Johnson's used to doing the pushing, not vice versa."

"The bigger they are," Starbuck said stolidly, "the harder they fall."

Stimson munched his cigar, nodded wisely. "If you don't mind my asking, what's your name?"

Starbuck gave him a wooden look. "Lee Hall."

"Uh-huh." Stimson's expression was one of veiled disbelief. "Where do you call home, Mr. Hall?"

"Texas." Starbuck took a slow drag, exhaled smoke. "New Mexico. I drift around."

"What's your line of work?"

"Little of this and a little of that."

"Jack-of-all-trades, huh?"

"You ask a lot of questions."

"No offense," Stimson said quickly. "I was just impressed by the way you manhandled Johnson. I'm always on the lookout for a good bouncer."

Starbuck grinned ferociously. "I don't hire out. You might say I'm self-employed."

"Of course." Stimson chuckled a fat man's chuckle. "A little of this and a little of that."

"Beats working for a living."

"I suspect it does." Stimson heaved himself to his

feet. "Well, enjoy your stay in Virginia City, Mr. Hall."

"I intend to, Mr. Stimson. I shorely do."

Stimson nodded pleasantly and walked away. Starbuck laughed to himself, inwardly delighted with the evening's work. He thought things had gone even better than he'd planned. Lola would continue to ferret out choice tidbits on the local grapevine. Word of the drubbing he'd given Johnson would spread rapidly. Omar Stimson would doubtless let it drop he was using an alias and was a mite touchy about questions. All of which, lumped together, would fuel the impression he wanted circulated throughout Virginia City.

Lee Hall was a man slightly windward of the law.

Chapter Four

Starbuck spent the next three days prowling around town. Every mining camp, much like a river at flood tide, had hidden undercurrents. He meant to determine the order of things in Virginia City.

Starting uptown, he leisurely reconnoitered the camp. His job was made easier by virtue of the brawl with Pete Johnson. The sporting crowd evidenced a strong dislike for Johnson, and not without reason. A bullyboy, overbearing and obnoxious, he was noted for throwing his weight around. According to Lola, the rumor was he'd been put out of commission for a week, perhaps longer. His jaw was broken and his gonads were swollen the size of gourds. The upshot was that Starbuck, in the guise of Lee Hall, had become the talk of Virginia City. The sporting crowd treated him with deference and applauded the neat job he'd made of Pete Johnson. He was welcome wherever he went.

The dives along Wallace Street proved to be a lode of information. Starbuck was a good listener and versed in the techniques of subtle interrogation. He concentrated on saloons and gaming dens, for these were the principal gossip mills of any boomtown. He

talked with gamblers and pimps, bartenders and grift-
ers, and what seemed a legion of ordinary miners.
Once they were engaged in conversation, he guilefully
prompted them along with rapt interest and a few
leading questions. Upon parting, he knew virtually
everything they knew, and no one the wiser. He
slowly pieced together the story of those hidden undercurrents.

John Duggan, president of the Virginia City Mining Association, was not altogether the civic partisan
he pretended. Nor was his concern over vigilantes
wholly altruistic. There was, instead, bad blood between Duggan and Wilbur X. Lott, the man behind
the vigilante movement. The problem stemmed from
economic conflict and opposing interests. Duggan was
the stalking horse for financiers and businessmen, the
growing cadre of mine owners. Lott, who worked his
own claim on Daylight Creek, was the self-appointed
champion of the independent miners. The collision
was all but ordained, one that sooner or later touched
every mining camp. Virginia City was merely the latest battleground.

All gold bonanzas, in the beginning, were strictly
surface operations. The gold was discovered above
ground, generally along creeks or rivers. The most
common method of extracting dust and nuggets from
loose earth was known as placer mining. The dirt was
shoveled into a rocker, which was nothing more than
a crude sluice box. The whole affair was rocked back
and forth while water moved the material down a series of flumes. Since gold was heavier than dirt, it
dropped to the bottom and was trapped there. A placer

miner needed little more than a strong back and some ordinary tools. His claim was his ticket to independence. He worked it himself, and *all* the dust went into his poke.

Quartz mining, on the other hand, was the search for gold below ground. A tunnel was sunk in the earth, or burrowed into a mountain, and followed the vein wherever it traveled. The tunnel was shored with wooden beams, and the quartz was dislodged from the earth with blasting powder. Then the loose quartz was run through an ore crusher to separate the gold. The process required stamp mills and heavy equipment, and men to work the mines. Which in turn required enormous amounts of capital, and investors. There was, moreover, the need to acquire surrounding claims; only in that manner could the vein be followed and the investment protected. Complicated and costly, it was a game that attracted wealthy businessmen and moneyed entrepreneurs. Once quartz mining began, it generally tolled the death knell for placer miners. There was no room for small operators when the stakes were boosted sky-high.

So the lines were now drawn. On one side stood John Duggan and the members of the mining association. On the other stood Wilbur X. Lott and the independent miners. The two sides were at loggerheads, and there would be no compromise. The robbers, in effect, were being used as the catalyst in a power struggle. The real issue was control of Virginia City and untold millions in gold. The vigilante movement was merely an outgrowth of that conflict. A fight between the little dog and the big dog over a bone. A golden bone.

Starbuck was hardly surprised. Always the cynic, he knew that men's motives were seldom what they appeared. Ambition and greed were often cloaked in the pious rhetoric of do-gooders. Yet his curiosity about the vigilantes had led quite naturally to questions about the robbers, and there he was surprised. All he'd heard tended to confirm what Lola had told him. No one gang was thought to be responsible for the robberies. Nor was there the slightest hint of a he-wolf gang leader. The general consensus was that cutthroats and robbers infested the countryside. It was considered to be a murderous form of free enterprise, with devil take the hindmost.

The thought occurred that he was somehow being used by John Duggan and the mining association. Then, upon reflection, he concluded it was unlikely. Horace Griffin, the Wells Fargo superintendent, was not easily hoodwinked. Nor was Munro Salisbury, the stageline owner, a man given to jumping at shadows. In their opinion, one gang was responsible for the express-shipment holdups. That in no way discounted the possibility that other robbers were preying on lone miners. Their belief, quite simply, was that the number of stage holdups almost certainly indicated an organized gang and a Judas. For all he'd heard to the contrary, Starbuck still agreed with their argument. Some inner voice told him it was so.

One other point seemed beyond dispute. Sheriff Henry Palmer was apparently a hell-on-wheels lawman. Apart from the robbers he'd captured—and hanged—he had personally killed four outlaws in gunfights. The common wisdom, expressed by miners as well as the sporting crowd, tagged him a resourceful and dedicated peace officer. At the same time, everyone thought he was faced by staggering odds. His war on the criminal element, despite a full complement of deputies, was hampered by the mountainous terrain and the sheer number of outlaws. While it was an uphill battle, his efforts had brought accolades from as far away as the territorial capital. The attorney general of Montana had nominated him for the post of U.S. marshal. The honor had boosted his reputation yet another notch in Virginia City.

Starbuck briefly considered contacting the sheriff. Then, on second thought, he rejected the idea. When working undercover, he seldom revealed himself to local peace officers. Some were resentful and jealous of outsiders, and others were simply more hindrance than help. There were exceptions, but those were lawmen Starbuck knew personally. They belonged to a loose confederation of peace officers he corresponded with regularly, and all of them had contributed in some fashion to his rogues' gallery. Even with them, however, he exercised great caution. Too many men liked to hear themselves talk, and a slip of the lip might very well imperil his life. So he was doubly cautious about Henry Palmer. There were too many factions at work in Virginia City, and the sheriff was still an unknown quantity. All in all, a lone hand seemed the wiser option.

By his third day in town, Starbuck was forced to admit he was stymied. He had unearthed a great deal

of interesting, and sometimes intriguing, information.
But none of it was especially germane to his investigation. Nothing he'd uncovered thus far shed any light
on either the gang or the gang leader. In fact, everything he had learned tended to obscure an already
murky situation. He decided to let it rest for a couple
of days. He was by now a familiar figure around the
camp, and he'd managed to get thick with the sporting
crowd. Sooner or later someone would say something
worth hearing, and his years as a manhunter had
taught him a vital lesson. Only the killing was done
swiftly. The stalk should never be rushed.

Every evening he made it a practice to drop by the
Gem Theater. He stayed only for one show, and he
never attempted to monopolize Lola's time. She
joined him at his table, and for appearance's sake he
always ordered a bottle of champagne. They laughed
and flirted, and so far as anyone could tell, he was
simply one of her many admirers. She related whatever she'd learned during the day, and once the champagne was finished it was generally time for the
second show. He then tried his hand at faro or went
on to another dive. Thus far, he had steered clear of
her hotel room, restricting all contact to the theater.
He was still leery of arousing suspicion.

Tonight, as was his habit, Starbuck drifted into the
Gem as the first show got under way. Stimson greeted
him jovially and ushered him to a ringside table. A
waiter quickly materalized with a bottle of champagne
and two glasses. Starbuck lit a smoke and settled back
to enjoy the show. Lola sang a couple of sultry bal-
lads, all alone onstage, the house gone quiet as a

church. Then a chorus line pranced out of the wings, and she led them in a rollicking, sometimes bawdy, dance number. The crowd gave her a thunderous ovation, and she disappeared with one last flash of her magnificent legs. The next act, a team of acrobats, romped out to mild indifference. The Gem's clientele wasn't much on gymnastic feats.

A short while later Lola appeared from backstage. She wandered through the audience, pausing here and there to chat a moment and accept congratulations. Then, fending off a drunken miner, she made her way to Starbuck's table. He rose with a courtly bow and held out her chair. She favored him with a beguiling smile.

"Good evening, Mr. Hall."

"Miss Lola." Starbuck seated himself and poured champagne. "You sure wowed 'em tonight! Yessir, that was some show."

"Aren't you sweet!"

"Compliments come easy where you're concerned, Miss Lola."

"You sly rogue!" Her voice suddenly dropped. "God, I couldn't wait to get out here! I'm onto something, lover. Something important!"

"Stay cool!" Starbuck cautioned. "Half the people in this joint are still eyeballing you."

Lola laughed as though he'd said something marvelously amusing. "I've been bringing the musicians along slow and easy. They're all boozers and the biggest gossips in the world. Just before the show, one of them got me aside on the q.t. and gave me an earful. I mean the lowdown!"

"Let's hear it."

"Have you ever heard of Doc Carver?"

"Not that I recollect."

"Well, hold on to your hat, lover! You won't forget him after tonight."

"Is he a local man?"

"No," Lola said softly. "He's a sharpshooter. You know, one of those trick-shot artists. Stimson brought him here early this summer for a limited engagement. But his act was so popular he was held over almost two months."

"So what's that got to do with anything?"

"Only this," Lola replied, her tone low and urgent. "His daughter was murdered."

"Daughter?" Starbuck looked confused. "You just lost me."

"She was part of the act! Carver shot cigarettes out of her mouth and all those other routines sharpshooters do. From what I gather, she was a real beauty. Gave the act a touch of class!"

"Why was she murdered?"

"Now it gets interesting!" Lola's face was animated, eyes flashing. "My musician friend says she got in over her head. She learned something she wasn't supposed to know, and it got her killed."

"What was it she learned?"

"Nobody knows." Lola collected herself, casually took a sip of champagne. "Here's the topper, though! The rumor's all over town it had something to do with the stage robberies."

"Any names?" Starbuck demanded. "Some idea as to who killed her?"

"Not a peep," Lola said ruefully. "There was talk that she was having an affair—"

"Wait a minute!" Starbuck broke in. "You mean she was sleeping with somebody?"

"So everyone thought! But no one had any inkling of who, or where she met him, or anything else. She was a very secretive little lady!"

"When was she killed?"

"Not quite a month ago."

"What happened to her father?"

Lola's eyes danced merrily. "He took off like a ruptured goose! Everyone thinks he knew who did it and why—and skipped town to save his own neck!"

"If he knew so much, then why wasn't he killed?"

"Search me, lover! I'm just telling you what I was told."

Starbuck mulled it over a moment. "Any idea where he skipped to?"

"Believe it or not—" Lola laughed. "He joined Buffalo Bill's Stage Show!"

"Bill Cody?"

"The one and only!" Lola bobbed her head. "There was an item in the paper. He went straight as a bumblebee from here to North Platte, Nebraska. Cody's theatrical troupe headquarters there."

"I'll be go to hell!"

"Will it help? Does it give you a lead of any kind—a clue?"

"I don't know," Starbuck said slowly. "I'll have to think on it."

"Well, I've got another show to do. Will you wait

on me? I damn sure don't want to be kept in suspense
until tomorrow night!"

"Tell you what." Starbuck hoisted his glass, pretended to toast her. "You go on to the hotel after the
show. I'll meet you in your room."

"Goody, goody! Looks like my lucky night!"

Lola downed her champagne and hurried backstage. Starbuck sat like a dreamy vulture, staring off
into space. After a while, he rose from his chair and
dropped a double eagle on the table. His expression
was still bemused.

He walked from the theater as the band thumped
to life.

Lola entered the hotel shortly after midnight. One of
the Gem's bouncers had escorted her from the theater.
His presence ensured that she would not be bothered
by late-night drunks and rowdies on the street. He saw
her into the lobby, then bid her good night. She waved
to the desk clerk and swiftly mounted the stairs.

On the second floor, she proceeded along the hallway to her room. She unlocked the door and stepped
inside. A match flared in the darkness, and she uttered
a sharp gasp. Chuckling softly, Starbuck lit a table
lamp, trimmed the wick low. She locked the door and
turned to face him. Her voice was shaky.

"You scared the living bejesus out of me!"

"Sorry." Starbuck dropped into one of the chairs
beside the table. "I wanted to avoid being seen. Figured the odds were better if I let myself in before you
arrived."

"So you picked the lock?"

"One of my minor talents." Starbuck motioned to the other chair. "Come sit down. We've got some talking to do."

Lola tossed her cape on the bed and crossed to the chair. She studied his dour expression a moment. "Why do I get the feeling it's bad news?"

"Not bad, exactly," Starbuck remarked. "But there's been a change of plans. I have to go to North Platte."

"Omigawd!" Lola yelped. "You're going after Doc Carver!"

"Got no choice." Starbuck's square features creased with worry. "I've thought it through, and it's the only way. Unless I got lucky, I could hang around here till doomsday before I turned up a lead. A talk with Carver might do the trick *muy pronto*."

"Then you believe it—about him and his daughter?"

"I believe she was murdered. Whether or not it had anything to do with the robbers—" Starbuck lifted his hands in a shrug. "I reckon I'll have to let Carver tell me that."

"Why else would he have run?"

"That's got me puzzled." Starbuck massaged his jaw. "Apparently it's pretty common knowledge he joined Cody's show. So if somebody was afraid he'd spill the beans, why not go to North Platte and kill him? He's just as much a threat there as he was here."

"Maybe the robbers—the gang leader—didn't read the paper."

"Maybe," Starbuck conceded. "Guess I won't know till I ask."

Lola cocked her head to one side. "What makes you think he'll talk? After all, his daughter was murdered and he hasn't spoken up yet. He might tell you to take a hike!"

Starbuck smiled. "I'll reason with him."

"God help him!" Lola said with feigned horror. "When do you leave?"

"The end of the week," Starbuck told her. "We'll leave right after you finish your engagement at the Gem. That way, I'll know you got out of here safe and sound."

"Oh, for—"

"No argument!" Starbuck halted her protest with an upraised palm. "You're not staying here alone. I've already made up my mind, and the discussion's closed!"

"You're a worrywart! I'm perfectly capable of looking after myself!"

"Only one trouble." Starbuck was deadly earnest. "You've got a taste for undercover work and you're good at it. If I left you here, you'd keep on digging. I won't take that chance."

"Don't be too sure!" Lola's lips curved in a teasing smile. "I didn't have time to tell you everything tonight. You might want me to stick around . . . when you hear about Stimson."

"Stimson?" Starbuck returned her gaze steadily. "What about him?"

"He's a crook!" Lola announced. "You remember the musician who told me about Doc Carver? Well, he also told me that Stimson controls the vice in Virginia City. The gambling dives, the whorehouses, everything! They all pay a percentage off the top, or else they don't operate. Stimson's word is law, and he runs things with an iron fist!"

"Your musician friend?" Starbuck said wonderingly. "How come he blabs everybody's secrets to you? That's the part I'd like to hear."

"Oh, call it a woman's wiles!" Lola gave him a sexy wink. "I told you I have a way with men. And, sweetie, it sure makes undercover work easier. God, does it ever!"

"All the more reason to get you out of here! You're liable to put the whammy on the wrong man and wind up in hot water."

"What about Stimson?" Lola implored. "I'm positive he'd extend my engagement another week! Let me stay, and I'll bet anything I get the goods on him. I just know it!"

"No soap," Starbuck said stubbornly. "You leave on the same stage with me."

"Spoilsport!" Lola stuck out her bottom lip. "You're passing up the chance to blow this town wide open. And I'm the girl who could do it!"

"You're forgetting one thing."

"What's that?"

"I wasn't hired to get Stimson. I'm after a gang of robbers . . . not some sleazy vice boss."

"Well—" Lola replied with a charming little shrug. "It would have been fun, anyway. And besides, he's such an oily bastard he deserves to get caught!"

"Got you hooked, doesn't it?"

"Hooked?"

"Undercover work," Starbuck observed dryly. "You act like a kid turned loose in a candy store."

Lola stood and languidly moved to his chair. She sat down in his lap, encircled his neck with her arms. Her voice was furry velvet and she put her mouth to his ear.

"Luke?"

"Um-hum?"

"Would you let me work with you again . . . on another case?"

"I might."

"Promise?" she purred. "Cross your heart?"

"Think it'd be worth my while?"

"Why don't I give you a sample and let's see?"

"Sounds fair to me."

Lola extinguished the lamp. She kissed him and her tongue darted inside his mouth. She squirmed her bottom into his groin and felt his manhood harden. Her hand drifted like a tingling snowflake down his chest, then went lower still. She slowly unbuttoned his pants.

Starbuck suddenly rose and carried her to bed.

Chapter Five

Starbuck pulled into North Platte on the afternoon train. The Union Pacific depot was large and sprawling, constructed of brick. A two-story hotel abutted the rear of the station house, with a wing extending eastward. He went inside and took a room for the night.

The trip from Virginia City had consumed the better part of a week. By stage and train, he and Lola had made their way to Denver. There he'd laid over a night and then caught the northbound for Wyoming. At Laramie, he had switched to the Union Pacific and continued on to Nebraska. The roundabout route was tedious and wearing. Yet, for all the inconveniences, it had relieved him of a major worry. Lola's brief stint as an undercover operative had ended with her engagement at the Gem Theater. She was once more safely in Denver.

No longer in disguise, Starbuck registered at the hotel under his own name. He was pressed for time, and he thought it would speed things along if he approached Carver openly. After dropping his warbag in the room, he returned to the lobby. His inquiry about Buffalo Bill's theatrical headquarters was apparently routine stuff in North Platte. The desk clerk simply pointed him in the right direction, noting it was a short walk. Outside, he turned west on Front Street.

The town's main thoroughfare bordered the railroad tracks. Once a frontier outpost, the settlement had expanded along the banks of the South Platte River. A cavalry cantonment, Fort McPherson, was the hub of the community. The business district was centered on the fort, and behind it, toward the river, was a growing residential area. Stores and shops lined Front Street, but North Platte was still very much a small town. A brisk walk in any direction ended on open prairie.

Some distance past the fort, Starbuck stopped before a modest frame house. To the rear was a large barn and a log corral. A group of men, dressed in range clothes and vaquero costumes, was standing outside the barn. Several Indians were squatting in a patch of shade near the corral. Their faces were smeared with war paint, and their manner of dress pegged them as Pawnees. All of them looked like actors in a traveling stock company.

Starbuck circled the house and walked toward the barn. The loafers standing outside gave him a quick once-over, then went back to talking. He entered through the wide double doors and found himself in what appeared to be an office. The front of the barn had been partitioned off, and two men were busily at work. One was seated behind a table littered with correspondence and ledgers. The other sat at a rolltop desk, scribbling furiously with pen and paper. The wall behind them was emblazoned with show posters. Among the more eye-catching were advertisements for *The King of Border Men* and *The Scouts of the Plains*. All of them depicted Buffalo Bill in epic proportions.

The man behind the table glanced up. "Do something for you?"

Starbuck approached and halted. "I'd like to see Doc Carver."

"He's out."

"How about Bill Cody?"

"He's busy."

"Tell him it's important."

"I handle important matters for Colonel Cody."

"Who are you?"

"John Burke, manager of the company."

"Then you won't do." Starbuck's tone was flat and hard. "Suppose you just tell Cody I'm here."

"Now—" Burke hesitated, looked deeper into the pale stare. "What's the name?"

"Luke Starbuck."

"He doesn't like interruptions . . . but I'll try."

"You do that."

Burke stood and moved to a door at the end of the room. He rapped once and entered. The other man turned from his desk, watching Starbuck a moment. Then he dropped his pen and rose, walking forward.

"Are you *the* Luke Starbuck—the detective?"

"Usually," Starbuck acknowledged. "You've got the advantage on me."

"Oh!" The man smiled sheepishly. "I'm Prentiss

Ingraham, Mr. Starbuck. I write all of Bill's adventure stories."

Starbuck was familiar with the product, if not the man. It was common knowledge that one or more ghostwriters churned out the dime novels about Buffalo Bill. The stories were pure invention, written in a florid style, and pandered to the public's taste for hair-raising derring-do. The plots generally subjected Buffalo Bill to capture by savage Indians or desperados; by some ingenious trick he always managed to foil the villains and emerge victorious. A great many people accepted the stories as literal truth.

Around Denver, where Cody's stage show had appeared several times, he was known as See Me Bill. The nickname derived from his flamboyant style of dress and his passion for telling big windies about himself. His official autobiography, published not quite two years ago, merely served to reinforce the point. Westerners were now of the opinion that he was no longer able to distinguish between the dime-novel yarns and the reality of his years on the Plains. Starbuck, for his part, saw it as a sad commentary. He knew that Cody had served as chief of scouts for several cavalry regiments and had been awarded the Medal of Honor for bravery in action. He thought the truth far more compelling than the fiction.

"I've read a couple of your stories," Starbuck remarked, nodding toward the desk. "You writing a new one?"

"No, not a novel," Ingraham explained. "I'm working on a new play. We open in Chicago week after next, and from there we tour the East. Bill always insists on something fresh—original—to kick off the season."

"How do you keep coming up with ideas?"

Ingraham grinned and tapped his head. "All a product of the imagination! Our audiences like them wild and woolly!"

Starbuck couldn't argue the point. For the past decade, the Buffalo Bill Combination had toured America. The stage shows were a mix of vaudeville and melodrama. The shooting exhibitions and roping acts were generally a prelude. The feature attraction was a play starring Bill Cody, some farfetched tale involving danger and damsels in distress. The show was booked solid every year, and every performance played to a full house. Buffalo Bill was by now an institution, almost a household word. Theater owners considered his show money in the bank.

"What we do," Ingraham went on, "doesn't compare with your work, Mr. Starbuck. I've followed your cases in the newspapers, and I must admit I'm fascinated by the detective business. Have you ever considered doing an autobiography?"

"If I do," Starbuck said with a note of irony, "I'll look you up, Mr. Ingraham. You did a helluva job for Cody."

"Oh, no, you're mistaken! Bill wrote that himself!"

"In here, Mr. Starbuck." Burke reappeared in the doorway. "Colonel Cody will see you now."

Starbuck smiled at Ingraham and turned away. He crossed the room, moving past Burke, and stepped into an inner office. The walls were decorated with Indian regalia and all manner of weapons, and several overstuffed chairs were grouped around a long table. As Starbuck entered, two men rose from their chairs. One of them he immediately identified as Bill Cody.

Buffalo Bill looked the part of a hero. He was easily six feet tall, with broad shoulders and the straight-arrow carriage of a soldier. He wore a goatee and mustache, and his hair hung in ringlets over his shoulders. He was attired in fringed buckskins and knee boots, and a brace of ivory-handled pistols were strapped around his waist. He grinned broadly and extended his hand.

"Welcome, Mr. Starbuck!"

"I appreciate your time, Mr. Cody."

Starbuck sensed he was somewhat ossified. Cody's eyes were slightly glazed and his breath smelled of liquor. All of which seemed to confirm his reputation as a boozer. Still, he was in dazzling good humor and clearly delighted by the interruption. He shook Starbuck's hand vigorously.

"I don't mind saying it's a pleasure to meet you, Mr. Starbuck! You are the premier detective of our fabled West! God strike me dead if you're not!"

Starbuck brushed aside the compliment. "Every cripple does his own dance."

"You're too modest!" Cody motioned the other man forward. "Let me introduce you to someone who chronicles the deeds of men such as ourselves. Luke Starbuck, meet Edward Judson. Otherwise known as Ned Buntline!"

"Mr. Starbuck." Buntline pumped his arm. "I've been an admirer of yours for years."

Starbuck was mildly surprised. A writer by trade,

Buntline was perhaps the best-known dime novelist of the day. There were many people who credited him as well with Bill Cody's success. Some years ago they had teamed up to produce the original stage show and several Buffalo Bill dime novels. Then, by all accounts, Cody had severed the partnership and sent Buntline packing. The writer's presence today made for interesting speculation.

"Don't stand on formality!" Cody trumpeted. "You boys grab a chair!"

"I wonder—" Starbuck stopped him with a gesture. "Would it be possible to speak with you in private? I don't mean to intrude, but it's important."

"You're not intruding!" Cody assured him. "We were just sitting around chewing the fat. Weren't we, Ned?"

Buntline got the hint. "Why don't I check with you later, Bill? That will give you time to think things over."

"Capital idea!" Cody agreed. "I'll sleep on it overnight."

"Tomorrow, then." Buntline glanced at Starbuck. "Hope to see you again, Mr. Starbuck."

Cody ushered him to the door with an arm around his shoulders. Buntline paused, talking quietly a moment, then went out. Cody firmly closed the door and turned back into the room.

"You showed up just in the nick of time, Mr. Starbuck."

"Oh?" Starbuck inquired. "How so?"

"That sorry bastard come all the way out here from New York! Since we busted up, his luck turned sour and he's looking for a meal ticket. He's got some damnfool notion I'll take him back."

"And you won't?"

"Never!" Cody struck a dramatic pose. "Nothing personal, you understand. We had what might be termed an artistic difference of opinion. Ned always ignored the facts of my life on the Plains! He chose to write plays that presented me as some godlike creature. Absolute tommyrot!"

"Whereas you wanted to tell it the way it happened?"

"Exactly!" Cody said in an orotund voice. "I believe in realism, Mr. Starbuck. I want the public to experience it as though they were there. I have a reputation to maintain!"

For Starbuck, any lingering doubts were dispelled. Cody had clearly fooled himself, lost touch with reality. He genuinely believed that Bill Cody the scout and Buffalo Bill the legend were one and the same. He saw himself as that intrepid hero depicted in the dime novels. It was self-deception at its worst, and almost laughable. The man standing before him was no longer Bill Cody. He was, instead, an illusion. The product of some hack writer's dizzy fantasies.

"I see your point," Starbuck said with a straight face. "Too bad Buntline lives in a dreamworld."

"Well, enough of my problems! Sit yourself down—can I call you Luke?—I never was much on ceremony."

"Sure thing, Bill." Starbuck smiled to himself, took a chair. "So far as I'm concerned, *Mister* was something folks called my dad."

"My sentiments exactly!" Cody said, seating himself. "Now, what can I do for you. Luke? I'd guess you're not here on a social visit."

"Your manager—Burke—didn't he tell you?"

"God, no! Burke wouldn't say 'boo' in front of Buntline. No love lost between those two!"

"Tell you the truth, I didn't want to say too much in front of Burke. What brought me here's a little delicate . . . confidential."

"I respect a confidence," Cody intoned. "Anything you say goes no further!"

"Figured as much," Starbuck said equably. "Just between us—I need to have a talk with Doc Carver."

"By jingo!" Cody's brow furrowed. "Is Carver in trouble with the law?"

"Nothing like that." Starbuck dismissed the idea with a wave of his hand. "When I asked outside, Burke told me Carver's not here. So I thought you could put me in touch."

"I'm afraid Burke misled you. Carver's not here—not on the property—but he's in North Platte. He has a suite at the hotel."

"The hotel?" Starbuck repeated. "Well, that takes a load off my mind. I started to think he'd flown the coop."

"Flown—" Cody stopped, frowning heavily. "Then he is in trouble!"

"What makes you say that?"

"I was a lawman myself once! Guess I've still got a nose for it when something smells fishy."

"I'll be dipped!" Starbuck prompted him. "So you actually wore a star?"

"U.S. deputy marshal!" Cody said proudly. "That was back in Kansas, the spring of '68. Some soldier boys deserted and stole a bunch of horses from the army. Bill Hickok and me tracked 'em all the way to Colorado and nabbed the whole gang. Killed three and brought back eleven prisoners!"

"You mean to say you worked with Wild Bill himself?"

"Other way around," Cody corrected him. "Hickok worked with me! I asked the army to deputize him and send him along as my assistant. That's how he got his start as a peace officer."

"Think of that!" Starbuck marveled. "You and Wild Bill!"

Cody preened like a peacock. "A good man and a stout friend! I taught him everything I knew, and he went on to become one of the great marshals of the West. Yessir, we made quite a team in the old days!"

Starbuck suspected it was all a windy tale. Yet Cody's garrulous bragging abruptly resolved another question in his mind. He'd been stalling, wondering how much he should reveal about Doc Carver. Now he decided the less said the better. No secret was safe with Buffalo Bill Cody.

"That's a mighty interesting story, Bill. Wish I had more time to jawbone, but time's awasting. I reckon I'd best be on my way."

"Hold on!" Cody said quickly. "I got myself sidetracked, and you never told me about Carver."

"Now that you mention it," Starbuck countered, "a minute ago you said you smelled something fishy. What'd you mean?"

"Oh, call it a hunch," Cody said with a shrug. "Carver's been off his feed lately. I just figured it had something to do with Virginia City."

"Virginia City?" Starbuck's look betrayed nothing. "I don't follow you."

Cody spread his hands in a bland gesture. "Carver finished an engagement there last month. I jumped to the conclusion he'd got himself in Dutch with the law."

"Couldn't prove it by me," Starbuck said, rising to his feet. "I'm here to get a deposition in a civil suit. Course, I'm not at liberty to disclose the details. You'll have to ask Carver about that."

"Maybe I will," Cody said absently. "I only asked because I wanted to make damn sure he'll be available next summer."

"What happens next summer?"

"Great thundering cannonballs!" Cody boomed jovially. "You haven't heard, have you? That's when the world gets a gander at my new Wild West Show!"

Starbuck appeared confounded. "What's a Wild West Show?"

"I'm quitting the stage!" Cody beamed. "P. T. Barnum has shown me the light! Last year he merged with James Bailey, and they're calling their circus the Greatest Show on Earth. Their first engagement was Madison Square Garden—and it was a sellout!"

"Yeah?" Starbuck was still bemused. "So what's that got to do with the West?"

"Spectacle!" Cody thundered gleefully. "The public wants spectacle and pageantry! That's exactly what I plan to give them. After this season, we're through with theaters. We'll play in outdoor arenas and circus tents, anywhere masses of people can be brought together. We'll make Barnum and his goddamn midget look like hayseeds!"

"Are you talking about a western circus?"

"Not bad, Luke!" Cody was caught up in a tempest of imagination. "Only it'll be more on the order of the old Roman circus. We'll have wild animals and trick-shot artists and all these new rodeo events. We'll have savage redskins and cavalry charges, and pitched battles on horseback. I tell you, it will revolutionize the show business!"

"A Wild West Show?" Starbuck shook his head, considering. "Yeah, I suppose something like that would go over big with easterners."

"It damn sure better!" Cody said with a rolling laugh. "Otherwise, I'll be scratching a poor man's ass. I've hocked my soul to put this show on the road!"

"Well, I wish you luck, Bill."

"I'm obliged, Luke. Good wishes from a man of your caliber means a lot! Wherever we're playing, you'll always be welcome. Buffalo Bill's personal guest!"

Starbuck thought it unlikely. He'd never had much use for showoffs and braggarts, men who forever sought the limelight. Their ways were foreign to him, and beneath their bravado he'd always detected something of the phony. Yet he found himself curiously ambivalent about Bill Cody. A scout who had won the Medal of Honor was no counterfeit hero.

Upon reflection, Starbuck decided the theatrics and the tall tales were a pardonable offense. He supposed there was room in the world for one See Me Bill. And a Wild West Show.

Chapter Six

On the way uptown Starbuck scarcely noticed passersby. His thoughts turned from Cody to Doc Carver. He mentally reviewed all he knew about the sharpshooter.

William Carver was an easterner and a former physician. Some years earlier he had abandoned his medical practice for a more lucrative career in show business. Shooting exhibitions were all the rage, and Carver possessed a natural gift with firearms. In 1878, using a rifle, he had captured the coveted title World's Champion Marksman. Glass balls were thrown into the air, and he'd broken 5,500 out of 6,211 tries. From there, he had gone on to exhibitions throughout America and Europe. He billed himself as the Evil Spirit of the Plains, trading on the world's fascination with the West. While he claimed to have fought in the Minnesota Sioux uprising, he had never fired a gun in anger. He was a sawbones turned showman.

Apart from those details, Starbuck possessed little in the way of hard intelligence. He knew Carver's daughter had been murdered, and he knew Carver had hastily departed Virginia City. The rumors surrounding those events were unsubstantiated and therefore of limited value. Few men broke under interrogation unless confronted with cold facts. So today's game of wits would rely largely on bluff. A liberal amount of conjecture flavored with a dab of truth.

At the hotel, Starbuck inquired Carver's room number. The desk clerk informed him it was a suite and pointed him upstairs. On the second floor, he turned left and walked to the end of the hall. He rapped on the door marked 230 and waited. Then he rapped harder.

Some moments passed before the door opened. The man facing him was slim and lithely built, with a brushy mustache. His eyes were steady and phlegmatic, and his features were hawklike. He looked anything but the coward.

"May I help you?"

"Dr. W. F. Carver?"

"Yes."

"I'm Luke Starbuck." Starbuck smiled genially. "Bill Cody said you might be able to spare me a few minutes."

"For what purpose?"

"A private matter."

"I see." Carver hesitated a beat, then swung open the door. "Come in."

"Thank you."

The suite was large and comfortably furnished. On other side of the parlor there were doors leading to separate bedrooms. A bay window provided a southern exposure, overlooking the river. The parlor was well appointed, with a sofa and three easy chairs.

Vases filled with wild prairie flowers were scattered around the room.

Carver closed the door and turned into the parlor. He motioned Starbuck to a chair. "What business do you have with Cody?"

"None." Starbuck placed his hat on a table, sat down. "I'm a private detective."

"Starbuck?" Carver took a seat on the sofa, suddenly nodded. "Why, of course! You're the investigator from Denver. I've read about you in the *Police Gazette*."

"Don't believe a word of it," Starbuck said affably. "Their reporters seldom bother to check the facts."

Carver chuckled politely, crossed his legs. "Well now, what brings you to see me, Mr. Starbuck?"

"Virginia City." Starbuck let him hang a moment. "I'm investigating a series of murders."

"I—" Carver paused, his expression guarded. "I don't believe I understand."

"Are you familiar with Mr. Wilbur X. Lott?"

"Anyone who's been to Virginia City has heard of Wilbur Lott."

"Then you know several miners have been murdered there recently. He hired me to look into the matter."

"I understood Lott was the moving force behind the vigilante movement. Why would he hire a private detective?"

"He needs proof," Starbuck lied, deadpan. "Before he hangs anybody, he wants the evidence to back his play."

"I find that rather astounding . . . to say the least."

"Why so?"

"Lott's a scoundrel!" Carver informed him stiffly. "Nothing more than a demagogue with political ambitions!"

"You seem well informed about Virginia City."

"A man like Wilbur Lott attracts attention. In fact, he takes great pains to keep himself in the public eye."

"I never judge a client," Starbuck observed neutrally. "I just do the job I was hired to do."

"In that case"—Carver's eyebrows drew together in a frown—"why have you come to me?"

"Your daughter was murdered there last month."

Carver blinked, licked his lips. "I fail to see the connection."

"Lott thinks the murders and the stage holdups are the work of one gang."

"What has that to do with my . . . daughter?"

"Everything," Starbuck said pointedly. "There's talk around Virginia City that your daughter got herself mixed up with the stage robbers."

"That's preposterous!" Carver laughed, but it didn't ring true. "The most absurd thing I've ever heard!"

"Some folks say your daughter was murdered because she learned too much for her own good."

"Idle gossip and speculation, nothing more!"

"It gets worse." Starbuck fixed him with a piercing look. "I don't know how to say it tactfully, Dr. Carver. Your daughter was having an affair with somebody—"

"A lie! A damnable lie!"

"—and that somebody was responsible for her death."

"How dare you!" Carver shouted. "Nothing of the sort ever happened. Never!"

"No?" Starbuck's tone turned curt and inquisitorial. "Then how come you took off running?"

"What?"

"You almost set your pants on fire getting out of Virginia City! Who scared you off?"

"Nobody!" Carver shook his head wildly. "Nobody scared me off!"

"You're lying!" Starbuck said roughly. "Somebody killed your daughter, and you hauled ass before he could kill you."

Carver went ghastly pale. "You don't know what you're talking about."

"Come off it!" Starbuck pressed him. "Don't you want your daughter's murderer caught and hung?"

"I refuse to listen any longer! I want you to leave, Mr. Starbuck. Now!"

Starbuck gave him a jaundiced stare. "You'll listen till I'm done talking, Carver. If you're not concerned about your daughter, then maybe you ought to worry about yourself. You're living on borrowed time."

Carver regarded him with profound shock. "What do you mean?"

"Stop and think about it!" Starbuck's voice was harsh, insistent. "Wherever you are, you're still a threat to the killer. Distance doesn't mean a damn thing! One of these days he'll wake up to the fact that you could still identify him and put his head in a noose. That's the day he'll track you down and kill you."

"You're wrong." Carver averted his gaze. "That will never happen."

"Stop kidding yourself!" Starbuck persisted. "You've only got one hope—and that's me!"

"You?" Carver made an empty gesture with his hands. "How can you help?"

"Tell me his name," Starbuck said grimly. "I'll find him and kill him. That way, you're off the hook for good."

A shadow of anxiety clouded Carver's features. He passed a hand across his eyes and swallowed hard. He opened his mouth to say something, then appeared to change his mind. Finally he took a deep breath and exhaled slowly.

"There's a lawyer in Virginia City."

"What's his name?"

"George Hoyt."

"He killed your daughter?"

"No," Carver said hesitantly. "But he can tell you things . . . names."

"Whose names?" Starbuck asked. "Your daughter's killer? The stage robbers?"

"I won't say any more, Mr. Starbuck. I've already said too much. Go back to Virginia City and talk to George Hoyt. He knows everything . . . all of it."

"You're talking in riddles!"

"I'm sorry." Carver screwed up his features in a tight knot. "I won't involve myself any further. That's all I have to say."

Silence thickened between them. After long deliberation, Starbuck's face took on a sudden hard cast. His tone was offhand, almost matter-of-fact.

"One last thing."

"Yes?"

"Don't shoot off a wire to anybody in Virginia City."

"Why would I do that?"

"Who knows?" Starbuck said coldly. "But if you warn anybody about our little talk . . . you're a dead man."

"You have no need to threaten me, Mr. Starbuck."

"Let's just call it a word to the wise."

The hallway door opened. A young girl stepped into the parlor, her arms laden with packages. As she turned to place the bundles on a nearby table Carver bounded off the sofa and hurried across the room. His expression was instantly jocular and his voice light-hearted.

"There you are, my dear!" He kissed her soundly on the cheek. "How was your shopping?"

"Oh, fine, considering the selection—"

"We have a visitor!" Carver took her elbow and steered her forward. "One of the West's most re-spected private investigators. Permit me to introduce Mr. Luke Starbuck."

Starbuck stood. "Pleasure to meet you, ma'am."

The girl was in her early twenties. She was slender and quite attractive, with hazel eyes and glossy auburn hair. Though built along dainty lines, she carried her-self erect and proud. Her smile was like a cameo come to life. She met Starbuck's gaze with a charming nod.

"Luke, this is Sally Devlin." Carver put his arm around the girl's waist and gave her a hug. "She's my new assistant. Joined the act after I returned from Virginia City."

"I'd say you did your act proud, Doc."

"Quite a bundle, huh?" Carver laughed and squeezed her tighter. "Don't know what I'd do without Sally! A pretty girl makes all the difference—in lots of ways!"

The girl blushed and dropped her eyes. Starbuck noted Carver's possessive attitude and thought it a cozy arrangement. She was easily half the sharpshooter's age, and he wondered how they'd got together. Then, just as quickly, he dismissed it from mind. Saloons and whorehouses were overrun with girls looking for escape. Sally Devlin wouldn't be the first to find it with an older man.

"Guess I'll be on my way, Doc."

"Luke, it's been a rare treat! Glad you could stop by."

Carver's jolly manner seemed wholly for the benefit of the girl. He walked Starbuck to the door and warmly shook hands. Then, at the last moment, he lowered his voice.

"Thanks for going along. I wouldn't want Sally to know anything about our talk. Might upset my love nest!"

"You just make sure you don't forget my word to the wise."

"I'm no fool, Luke. I heard you the first time."

Starbuck let go his hand and moved into the hall. Walking toward the stairs, his thoughts swiftly turned to Virginia City. And a lawyer named George Hoyt.

From the lobby, Starbuck headed for the hotel bar-room. He'd already decided to catch the morning westbound, and he reminded himself to check departure schedules. Yet he was still brooding on his conversation with Doc Carver. Something nagged at him, something he had overlooked.

Hard-won experience had taught him a vital lesson. Detective work was not altogether a matter of analytical reasoning. There was an element of instinct involved, and a man learned never to ignore those swift-felt impulses. His instinct told him he'd missed some critical lead while interrogating Carver. He couldn't put his thumb on it, and he was disturbed by the oversight. He thought a drink might wash away the cobwebs. A shot of popskull was known for its restorative effects.

The barroom was dim and pleasantly cool. The hour was early, and few of the tables were occupied. Only one man stood at the polished mahogany bar. Starbuck looked closer and saw that it was Ned Buntline. Too late, he tried to reverse course without being seen. Buntline spotted him and waved.

"Starbuck!" he called out. "Join me for a drink. I'm buying!"

Buntline was short and stocky, with bags under his eyes and sagging jowls. There was something baroque about him, even though his fingernails were gnawed to the quick and he had a nervous habit of twisting his mustache. The inveterate hustler, he was glib and clever, forever playing the angle. He was also a man with a checkered past.

Some years ago he had been caught bare-assed with another man's wife. He killed the husband in a duel and narrowly escaped being lynched by a mob. Later, following an altercation in New York's theater district, he had incited a riot. After being tried and convicted, he had spent a year in prison. Then, during the Civil War, he'd proved himself such a malcontent and troublemaker that he was eventually cashiered out of the Union Army. Upon returning to New York, he had at last found his true calling in life. He turned to purple prose and the printed page, where lies and chicanery were the accepted norm. He became a dime novelist.

Starbuck was aware of the details. Buntline's unsavory past had in turn been chronicled by the *Police Gazette* and several western newspapers. He wanted nothing to do with the writer, but he saw no way to avoid it. To decline a man's invitation was the worst of insults, and never done lightly. He agreed to one drink.

Buntline immediately launched into a tirade directed at Bill Cody. His tone was vituperative and his eyes blazed with resentment.

"Bastard!" he cursed sullenly. "After all I've done for him, you'd think he'd have a little gratitude!"

"Has he turned you down?"

"Not yet," Buntline said, his voice raw with bitterness. "But I see the handwriting on the wall. Tomorrow he'll give me the fast shuffle—so long and goodbye!"

Starbuck raised an uncertain eyebrow. "You figure he owes you something, that it?"

"He owes me everything!" Buntline replied angrily. "I *invented* Buffalo Bill Cody!"

"What do you mean . . . invented?"

Buntline laughed a tinny sound. "Before I took him underwing, he was just another dime-a-dozen army scout. I literally yanked him out of obscurity with the books and plays I wrote. I *sold* him to the public! I took a nobody and convinced America he was the white knight of the frontier. I made him famous—a legend!"

"Maybe so," Starbuck ventured. "Course, you had something to work with. A Medal of Honor winner isn't exactly a 'nobody.' "

"You think not?" Buntline said with wry contempt. "The true Scout of the Plains was a man named Frank North. The summer of '69, I came west to sign him up for a series of books. He turned me down cold, wouldn't touch it! So I looked around, and lo and behold, there stood Cody." He paused with a sourly amused look on his face. "Today Frank North's a nobody and Buffalo Bill's a national institution. You still think I didn't invent him?"

"If you did," Starbuck remarked succinctly, "then you should've stuck to the truth. These dime novels read like a kid's fairy tale. Nothing personal, but it's pure bullshit!"

"All history is bullshit," Buntline said, not in the least offended. "Whoever chronicles an event does so with an eye on posterity. Why should I be any different? I'm in the process of creating America's mythology! The fact that it's bullshit—based on false heroes—means nothing. A hundred years from now what I've written will be accepted as gospel truth. All mythology—Greek, Norse, Anglo-Saxon—was created the same way. Like it or not, legends aren't born . . . they're invented."

"Cody will be sorry to hear it."

"No, not Cody!" Buntline scoffed. "Most of the time he's so drunk he couldn't ride a hobbyhorse. He'll die believing his own press clippings!"

"Well, like you said," Starbuck commented, "you sold him to the public. I guess he's got to live up to his reputation."

A crafty look came over Buntline's face. "I could sell you twice as easy and twice as fast. Your reputation's the real article—documented fact!"

Starbuck squinted at him. "Are you offering to make me part of your mythology?"

"Why not?" Buntline's eyes crinkled with a smile. "In your case, there's no need for bullshit. You're a legend waiting to be born!"

"Thanks all the same." Starbuck wagged his head. "I reckon I'll have to pass."

"Stop and think!" Buntline admonished him. "Your autobiography alone would make a fortune! Add dime novels and stage appearances, and you'd end up ten times as famous as Cody. Don't you understand? You would *eclipse* Buffalo Bill!"

Starbuck tossed off his drink. "You ever tried to poke hot butter in a wildcat's ear?"

"I don't get your point."

"You write so much as a word about me and you'll get the point goddamn quick. Savvy?"

"Your loss, not mine." Buntline shrugged, sipped at his whiskey. "By the way, I meant to ask earlier. What brought you to North Platte?"

"Well, I got wind you were here. So I came all the way from Denver to give Cody a message."

"Oh?" Buntline eyed him warily. "What message was that?"

"You've heard about his Wild West Show?"

"Yes?"

"I told him there's no room in it for a butthole named Buntline."

Starbuck compounded the insult. He fished a cartwheel dollar out of his pocket and dropped it on the counter. Then he turned and walked from the barroom.

His smile was jack-o'-lantern wide.

Chapter Seven

The Virginia City stage rolled to a halt outside the express office. One of the passengers on top of the coach was a ragtag, down-at-the-heels miner. His features were hidden by a floppy slouch hat and a wild, matted beard. He looked like a cocklebur with eyes.

Starbuck climbed down off the stage. To all appearances, he was another in the horde of miners flocking to Alder Gulch. He wore an oversize mackinaw and he moved with the stoop-shouldered gait of someone broken by hard times. The phony beard, which was a customized theatrical prop, completed his disguise. He collected a worn carpetbag from the luggage boot and shuffled toward the boardwalk. He was all but invisible in the crowds thronging the street.

The disguise was essential to the plan he'd formulated. His interrogation of Doc Carver had confirmed a chain of events in the case. He had established a tenuous link between the Carver girl's murderer and the stage robbers. He had also uncovered the name of a potential informant, George Hoyt. The next step was to grill the lawyer and add still another link to the chain. Yet there was no certainty that Hoyt could be trusted. So the approach would be made in the guise of a scruffy miner. Afterward, Starbuck would resurrect the hardcase and drifter, Lee Hall. The switch in disguises would provide him freedom of movement wherever the case might lead. No one, including Hoyt, would be the wiser.

Starbuck prudently avoided the Gem Theater. He bypassed as well the Virginia Hotel, where he'd stayed while Lola was in town. Instead, he checked into a sleazy fleabag near the red-light district. He requested a room to himself and paid in advance. Upstairs, he sprawled out on the bed and caught a nap. The trip from North Platte had been long and tiring, and he wanted his wits about him tonight. Toward sundown, he rose and inspected his disguise in the washstand mirror. Then he went in search of George Hoyt.

The lawyer's office was on Van Buren Street. Starbuck found it by checking along side streets as he wandered through the heart of town. A wooden sign hung over the door and a shaft of lamplight spilled through the window. He walked past and saw a lone man seated at a desk. After checking the street in both directions, he felt reasonably confident he'd gone unobserved. He turned and retraced his steps. He went through the door without knocking.

The man looked up from a desk littered with paperwork and open law books. He was tall and gangling and wore wire-rimmed glasses. His eyes were magnified through thick lenses, and his features were somehow ascetic in appearance. He smiled pleasantly.

"May I help you?"

"Are you George Hoyt?"

"Yes, I am."

Starbuck locked the door and pulled the blind on the window. Then he moved forward and took a chair in front of the desk. Hoyt's eyes were large and wide behind the glasses, as though seen through the wrong end of a telescope. His expression was one of mild befuddlement.

"Why did you lock the door?"

"We need to have a talk . . . in private."

"Who are you?"

"What's in a name?" Starbuck watched him, alert to the slightest reaction. "I was sent here by Doc Carver."

All the blood leached out of Hoyt's face. His lips worked silently, and an odd furtiveness settled over his features. When at last he spoke, there was a faint catch in his voice.

"What do you want?"

"For openers"—Starbuck fixed him with a steady, inquiring gaze—"tell me about the Carver girl's murder."

Hoyt's mouth popped open. "If Carver really sent you, then why didn't he tell you himself?"

"I heard his version," Starbuck said gruffly. "Now I want to hear yours."

"Until you've identified yourself, I can't see why I owe you an explanation."

"Humor me." Starbuck studied him with icy detachment. "Otherwise, I'm liable to get mad and break your glasses."

Hoyt blinked, swallowed hard. Then he very gingerly nodded his head. "I was escorting Alice back to her hotel one night. It was quite late, and the street was empty. Someone fired from the shadows and missed me. Alice was killed . . . by mistake."

"Why would somebody want to murder you?"

"In addition to my law practice, I serve as the county prosecutor. I've sent several men to the gallows and made a great many enemies. Apparently one of them tried to assassinate me."

"The men you prosecuted," Starbuck asked, "were those the outlaws caught by Sheriff Palmer?"

"Yes."

"And you figure one of their friends tried to even the score?"

"It would appear so."

"Where had you been the night Alice Carver was killed?"

Hoyt looked acutely uncomfortable. "At my home."

"You said it was late . . . how late?"

"A little after three in the morning."

Starbuck played a hunch. "You were having an affair with her, weren't you?"

"I loved her," Hoyt confessed. "I still do. What happened between us is none of your business."

"Maybe." Starbuck eyed him in silence a moment. "Let's go back to the killer. How was he tied in with robbers?"

"I didn't say he was."

"We both know different, don't we?"

"You're putting words in my mouth!"

"Like hell!" Starbuck said curtly. "What was his name?"

"I have no idea."

"Doc Carver says you do."

"Thats impossible!" Hoyt blurted. "It was dark and I never saw anyone. Carver knows that!"

"He's changed his mind. He thinks it was somebody connected with the robbers."

"Thinking doesn't make it so!"

"Don't spar with me!" Starbuck's jawline tightened. "Carver's convinced the killer was one of the gang. Maybe even the gang leader himself."

"Gang leader?" Hoyt's forehead blistered with sweat. "Carver's crazy! I know nothing of any gang!"

Starbuck was gripped by a strange feeling. Some complex of instinct and experience told him the lawyer wasn't lying. Yet there was an underthought struggling to take shape in his mind. He tried to focus on it, quickly give it form and meaning, but he drew a blank. He put it aside and returned to the interrogation.

"How come Carver believes there's a gang?"

"I'm afraid you'd have to ask him."

"I'm asking you!" Starbuck regarded him dourly. "And I want an answer . . . now."

Hoyt avoided his gaze. "I can't tell you what I don't know."

Starbuck examined his downcast face. "All right, let's try another tack. You said you're the county prosecutor?"

"That's correct."

"So you have considerable dealings with Sheriff Palmer?"

"Yes, I do."

"What's his opinion?" Starbuck demanded. "Does he think there's a gang?"

"Not one gang," Hoyt said lamely. "I seriously doubt anyone in town believes that."

"How about the stagecoach robberies?" Starbuck inquired skeptically. "Has Palmer ever indicated—even hinted—that he thought they were the work of one gang?"

"No," Hoyt replied vaguely. "Not to my knowledge."

"So Alice Carver's death was a mistake? Somebody was after you and got her instead. That's your story?"

An indirection came into Hoyt's eyes. "Yes, that's exactly how it happened. A tragic accident."

"And the gang wasn't involved?"

"Who are you?" Hoyt said, his voice clogged. "Why are you trying to make me admit something that never happened?"

"Doc Carver hired me." Starbuck paused, gave him a narrow look. "Whatever his reasons are, he decided your story's a load of hogwash. He sent me here to kill whoever murdered his daughter."

Hoyt stared at him, aghast. "I don't believe you! Carver's not that big a fool!"

"You're the fool," Starbuck countered. "You're holding out on me, and that could buy you a world of grief."

"I've told you the truth!"

"Not the whole truth," Starbuck pointed out. "Somebody killed Carver's daughter and threatened his life. That's why he hightailed it out of town. I think you know that somebody's name."

Hoyt pursed his lips as if his teeth hurt. "You will never make me believe you're working for Doc Carver. It just doesn't make sense!"

"Believe what you want," Starbuck said, getting up. "Only keep it to yourself. I wouldn't want anybody to know we had ourselves a chat."

"No one would listen even if I told them."

Starbuck walked to the door, then turned back. "I'll be around awhile. Don't let your lip slip, or you're liable to see me again."

"Very well," Hoyt said hollowly. "You have my word on it."

The door opened and closed, and Starbuck was gone. George Hoyt pulled out a handkerchief and mopped his forehead. Then he seemed to wilt, staring blankly at the door.

His eyes were rimmed with fear.

The Gem Theater was packed. The barroom was doing a brisk business, and large crowds were gathered around the gaming tables. Onstage, a juggler played to an indifferent audience.

Starbuck stood at the bar. Earlier, he'd returned to his seedy hotel room and performed a change in character. The miner's outfit, along with the phony beard, had gone into his carpetbag. Then he'd donned his old garb and plastered the handlebar mustache in place with spirit gum. Waiting until the desk clerk was busy, he had slipped out of the hotel unobserved. The carpetbag had been consigned to an alley trash heap, and he'd made his way to the Gem. He was now in the guise of Lee Hall.

Watching the show, he was aware of the looks from those around him. The fight with Pete Johnson was still remembered, and word would quickly spread that he was back in town. His purpose was to make himself visible and put the grapevine to work. Whatever he'd hoped to learn from George Hoyt, the grilling had proved a washout. He was convinced the lawyer had lied, but he was reluctant to push too hard too fast. He planned to wait a couple of days, allowing the pressure to build, and then try again. In the meantime, he would take another stab at his original scheme. He would let it be known that Lee Hall, the toughnut and drifter, was available. If there actually was a gang, the message would be passed along soon enough. All he could do was dangle the bait and await a nibble.

Omar Stimson, the Gem's owner, stopped by and bought him a drink. Starbuck played it mysterious about his absence from town. His response to Stimson's questions was a cryptic smile mixed with vague doubletalk. He left the impression he'd been involved in something slightly windward of the law.

While they were chatting, Pete Johnson walked through the door. He spotted Starbuck at the bar and halted in his tracks. Starbuck returned his glowering look with a wooden expression. The staring contest ended when Johnson blinked first. He turned on his heel and marched out the door with a stiff-legged stride. Starbuck chuckled softly.

"Guess he recollects our last go-round."

"Watch yourself," Stimson warned. "Johnson's a sore loser. He's been known to carry a grudge."

"That's his problem," Starbuck said lightly. "I don't look for trouble, but I'm always willing to oblige."

"Just thought I'd mention it."

"I appreciate the advice."

Stimson wandered off into the crowd. Starbuck had another drink, pleased by the incident. The vice boss of Virginia City apparently held him in some esteem. It was the sort of thing that would draw attention and thereby peg his reputation a notch higher. After finishing his drink, he decided to make the rounds. The more dives he visited, the faster the word would spread. And perhaps, with a little luck, he would get a nibble.

Outside the theater, he eased through a knot of miners ganged around the entrance. Then he stepped off the boardwalk and angled toward a gaming den on the far corner. He was almost to the middle of the street when a slug nicked the shoulder of his coat. A split second later the report of a gun sounded directly behind him. All thought suspended, he acted on reflex alone. He dodged sideways, pulling his Colt as a second bullet whistled past. Then he hit the ground in a rolling dive, dimly aware of men stampeding in every direction. On the third roll he spun himself about, flat on his belly. He thumbed the hammer and brought the sixgun to bear.

A third shot kicked dust in his face. He saw Pete Johnson standing in an alleyway, pistol extended at arm's length. Starbuck's finger feathered the trigger, and the Colt spat a sheet of flame. Then, with no more than a pulsebeat between shots, he emptied the gun. Johnson was driven backward as though struck by lightning. His arms windmilled crazily and the impact of the slugs sent him reeling in a strange, nerveless dance. He slammed into the wall of the theater; then his knees collapsed and he dropped his pistol. He pitched raglike to the ground. An eerie stillness settled over the street.

Starbuck pushed to his feet and began shucking empty shells. He reloaded as he walked to the alley. There he stopped and stood for a moment looking down at the body. All five shots were in the chest, less than a handspan apart. He grunted to himself and holstered the Colt. Then he caught a flicker of movement out of the corner of his eye. Omar Stimson stepped off the boardwalk and halted beside him.

"Looks like Johnson was feeling lucky."

"Sorry bastard!" Starbuck cursed savagely. "He tried to backshoot me!"

Stimson slowly inspected the blood-spattered corpse. He shook his head, whistled softly under his breath. "You're even better with a gun than you are with your fists."

"I generally get by." Starbuck paused, looked at him. "Guess I should've listened a little closer. You shore called the turn."

"You want some more advice?"

"Hell, why not?"

"Sheriff Palmer frowns on gunplay. Do yourself a favor and talk polite when he questions you."

"God a'mighty damn! It was self-defense, pure and simple!"

Stimson shrugged. "I'm just offering you a pearl of wisdom. Take it for what it's worth."

"You talk like he's some tough lawdog!"

"You will, too . . . when he's done with you."

Henry Palmer was a man with hard eyes and steel in his voice. He was trimly built, with dark wavy hair and a determined jaw. His bearing was monolithic, and he possessed a strong animal magnetism. He looked like someone accustomed to having his own way.

Starbuck was seated opposite him. On the sheriff's desk lay the Colt used to kill Pete Johnson. So far the questions had been general, almost conversational in tone. But now Palmer hefted the sixgun and studied it critically. The gutta-percha handles and lustrous blue finish gave it a distinctive appearance. He deftly unloaded the Colt and closed the loading gate. Then he eased the hammer to full cock and lightly touched the trigger. The hammer instantly dropped. He nodded and looked up.

"A hair trigger," he said quietly. "I would venture to say everything inside this pistol has been overhauled by a very competent gunsmith. Would I be wrong?"

"Search me," Starbuck said with a guileless smile. "I won it in a poker game."

"Who was your opponent . . . Doc Holliday?"

"You've got me all wrong, Sheriff!"

"No, Mr. Hall." Palmer's gaze bored into him. "Your shooting tags you for precisely what you are. You're a professional gunman!"

Starbuck rocked his hand, fingers splayed. "There's no law against a man protecting himself."

"In Virginia City"—Palmer's eyes were angry, commanding—"I am the law! A few weeks ago you whipped Johnson in a brawl, and tonight you killed him. That makes you a troublemaker in my book!"

"Johnson started it both times."

"So I've been told," Palmer said shortly. "Except for that, I'd have you under lock and key right now."

"I'm a mite confused, Sheriff." Starbuck's square face was very earnest. "Why'd you take my gun and haul me over here if you don't aim to arrest me?"

"Your habits interest me."

"Habits?" Starbuck repeated. "I don't get you."

"You were here for a week; then you disappeared for almost two weeks." Palmer paused with a speculative stare. "Now you're back . . . and nobody saw you arrive."

Starbuck gave him a walleyed look of amazement. "How'd you know all that?"

"I make it my business to know," Palmer said without inflection. "What I don't know is where you went—and what you did—when you left here."

"Any law says I gotta tell you?"

"No." Palmer's face grew overcast. "But there's a law you haven't heard about. I put it into effect and I enforce it."

"What law's that?"

"Everybody is entitled to one mistake. You made

yours by being too handy with a gun. Cause any more trouble, and I'll post you out of town."

"Oh?" Starbuck smiled crookedly. "Suppose you posted me and I took a notion to stay. What then?"

Palmer regarded him with clinical interest. "Then I'll kill you."

Starbuck let it drop there. His Colt was returned and he was allowed to leave. On the street, he paused and lit a cigarette, highly pleased with himself. He'd killed a man and he had put himself crosswise of Virginia City's badass sheriff. All in one night.

The word would spread like wildfire.

Chapter Eight

Starbuck awakened shortly before noon. He hadn't slept well, and his head felt groggy. He threw off the covers, sat for a moment on the edge of the bed. He dully recalled he was in the Virginia Hotel.

Last night, he'd gone straight from the sheriff's office back to the Gem Theater. His reception was even better than he had anticipated. Omar Stimson greeted him like a celebrity and insisted on buying several rounds of drinks. Killing a man—particularly Pete Johnson—had boosted his stock in Virginia City. The details were told and retold by those who had witnessed the shooting. He modestly allowed them to embroider on the truth.

From the Gem, Starbuck had made a tour of the dives along the street. The sporting crowd treated him something like a conquering hero. Strangers stood in line to shake his hand, and drinks were on the house. Before long, he'd consumed enough liquor to act the part of a drunken loudmouth. He began by bragging about the shootout; then he went on to relate the highlights of his standoff with the sheriff. By the end of the night, he had told the story no fewer than a dozen times. He finally called it quits, acting only slightly

drunker than he actually was, and checked into the
hotel. He was thoroughly satisfied with his performance. Lee Hall was the talk of the town.

Today, with a bright noontime sun streaming
through the window, his thoughts turned to other matters. As he shaved, it occurred to him that he was
somewhat impressed by Sheriff Henry Palmer. The
lawman was tough and resourceful, and he ran a tight
town. His credentials were in no way diminished by
the robberies and murders; his record of ten outlaws
hanged and four killed was noteworthy by any standard. He was, moreover, a deadly mankiller. Starbuck
recognized the breed on sight, for the quality was one
shared by all boomtown peace officers. The warning
issued by Palmer last night was no idle threat. Any
man posted out of Virginia City would be wise to
depart without delay. The alternative was to face the
sheriff—and be killed.

One thought led to another. Starbuck's ruminations
about the sheriff brought him once more to the matter
of George Hoyt. The lawyer's story was entirely plau-
sible; it was reasonable to assume the outlaws would
seek revenge against the county prosecutor. Yet, by
that yardstick, it was equally safe to assume the outlaws would have attempted to assassinate the sheriff.
And that wasn't the case. So Starbuck knew his instinct hadn't played him false. Hoyt had lied, and
there was no logical explanation to justify the lie. Despite his devious manner, the lawyer clearly wasn't in
league with the robbers. But if that was true, then the
lie seemed all the more unfathomable. Only one answer presented itself. Someone else, not the robbers,

had murdered the Carver girl. All of which led to a still greater riddle.

Who was George Hoyt protecting . . . and why?

Starbuck pondered the question as he dressed. Doc Carver was lying and George Hoyt was lying, and none of it made sense. He glued the mustache onto his upper lip, all the while searching for some rhyme or reason. At last, completely buffaloed, he walked to the bed and retrieved his pistol from beneath the pillow. He checked the loads and lowered the hammer on an empty chamber.

A knock sounded at the door. Starbuck crossed the room, his thumb hooked over the Colt's hammer. He stopped beside the doorjamb.

"Who's there?"

"I got a message for Lee Hall."

"Who from?"

"Lemme in and I'll tell you."

Starbuck twisted the key and backed to the center of the room. He leveled his sixgun on the door.

"C'mon in . . . slow and easy!"

The door creaked open. A tall, lantern-jawed man stepped into the room. He was grizzled and lean, with cold eyes and a tight-lipped expression. He looked like an undertaker at a funeral service, sober but not really sad. He closed the door and kept his hands in plain sight.

"I come in peace," he said solemnly. "You don't need no gun."

"Who're you and what's your business?"

"The name's Frank Yeager."

"I'm still listening."

"I got a proposition for you."

"What sort of proposition?"

"I don't talk so good lookin' down a gun barrel."

Starbuck wagged the pistol. "Take a seat on the bed. Put your hands on your knees and don't try anything sudden."

"Sudden ain't my game."

Starbuck waited until the man was seated. Then he pulled up a straight chair for himself and straddled it backward. He let the Colt dangle loosely in his hand.

"Awright, Mr. Yeager," he said churlishly. "What is your game . . . just exactly?"

"You killed Pete Johnson last night."

"So?"

"Johnson worked for me." Yeager's brow puckered with a frown. "Somebody's gotta fill his boots. I figgered you might be the man."

Starbuck was instantly attentive. "How do I know you're not trying to get even for Johnson? Sounds the least bit like a setup."

"If I wanted to kill you," Yeager observed, squinting querulously, "I'd just wait and bushwhack you some dark night. Why bother to rig a setup?"

"Guess you got a point," Starbuck conceded. "Course, it doesn't change things one way or the other. I got my own game and I play a lone hand."

"Yeah, I know." Yeager's eyes narrowed, and a smirk appeared at the corner of his mouth. "Word's around you snuck off and pulled a job last week."

Starbuck gave him the fisheye. "Where'd you hear that?"

"Little bird told me." Yeager laughed without humor. "I hear you're from Texas and you got no use for the law, and it's short odds your name ain't Lee Hall. I hear lots about you."

"Maybe too much," Starbuck bristled. "I never cared much for a man with a long nose."

"Don't get bent out of shape! Folks talk and I listen. No harm done!"

"Why all the interest in me?"

"You got guts!" Yeager grunted sharply. "And you damn sure ain't no tyro with a gun! Anybody that puts Pete Johnson away knows his business. So I figgered I'd sound you out."

"Since you don't hear so good, try watching my lips. I'm not for hire."

Yeager barked a short, harsh laugh. "You might change your tune when you hear the wages!"

"Try me and see."

"Anywheres from five to ten thousand a crack."

"Dollars?"

"Gold dust or dollars, it all spends the same."

Starbuck regarded him with a long, slow look. "What line of work are you in?"

"I rob stagecoaches."

There was a long pause of weighing and appraisal as the two men examined one another. At length, Starbuck fixed him with a corrosive stare. "Ten thousand? You wouldn't be pulling my leg, would you?"

"One way to find out," Yeager said simply. "Come along on a job and see for yourself."

"When did you have in mind?"

"You got a horse?"

"I could buy one easy enough."

"Not without everybody knowin' it." Yeager considered briefly, then nodded. "One of my men will come get you tomorrow night. He'll bring an extra horse."

"Where're we headed?"

"You'll see"—Yeager's eyes veiled with caution—"when we get there."

A fleeting look of puzzlement crossed Starbuck's face. "How'd you know I'd go for the deal? I could've turned you in to the sheriff and collected myself a reward."

"Four of my boys are waitin' outside the hotel."

"So what?"

"Unless they get the high sign from me, you'd be cold meat the minute you hit the street."

"You don't play for chalkies, do you?"

Yeager's mouth set in an ugly grin. "I only bet on sure things. You'll see what I mean the first trip out."

"Yeah, I reckon I will at that!"

"Okay if I get up now?"

"Jesus!" Starbuck stood with a foolish smile and quickly holstered his pistol. "I clean forgot I had you covered!"

"Well, don't forget tomorrow night. Somebody'll rap on your door right about dark."

"Frank, if you want a sure thing—bet on that!"

Starbuck walked him to the door and they shook hands. When Yeager was gone, he turned back into the room with a jubilant grin. The bait had been taken, hook and all! He'd got the invite he needed, and it had come from the gang leader himself. Which left only one question.

Who the hell was Frank Yeager?

• • •

An early September frost touched the land. In the valleys, where cottonwoods lined the creeks, a blaze of yellow foretold oncoming autumn. On the hillsides, columns of silver birch were flecked through with orange and gold. The air was sharp and crisp, and the mountains marched westward to the horizon. A brilliant sunrise lighted the pale sky.

The terrain got rougher as the men climbed steadily higher into the mountains. They followed the corduroy road that connected Virginia City with the railhead at Dillon. The steep grade was a series of hairpin curves and sudden switchbacks, twisting upward through the countryside. Frank Yeager led the way, and strung out behind him were five riders. The men wore mackinaws, and their horses puffed clouds of smoke in the frosty air. No one spoke.

Starbuck was the third rider in line. The other men were a coarse lot, hard and tough, still somewhat standoffish. He understood he was the new recruit, as yet untested. All the others were veteran highwaymen, old hands at robbery and murder. He'd been assigned the middle spot in the column, and it took no mental genius to figure the reason. He would be observed closely and entrusted with only the most menial chores. His every action would be noted, and his performance would determine his future with the gang. Today was a baptism into their ranks, and very much a test. It was his first job.

Four nights past, one of the gang had appeared at the hotel. His name was Charley Reeves, and he was

there at Yeager's order. He led Starbuck to the edge
of town, where two horses were hidden in a stand of
trees. They rode westward along a rutted wagon road,
and Reeves maintained an aloof silence the entire
way. Sometime after midnight, they forded a creek
and turned into the yard of a log house. Frank Yeager
greeted them at the door.

Over a jug of whiskey, Starbuck had been briefed
on the layout. Yeager operated a small cattle outfit,
located on Rattlesnake Creek. He supplied beef to
butcher shops in Virginia City, and he'd built a reputation as an honest rancher. In truth, the ranch was
nothing more than a clever front. The gang assembled
there before a robbery, and only then were they told
the details of the job. After the holdup, the loot was
split and the gang immediately dispersed. Since they
never returned to the ranch, there was no way to track
them from the scene of the robbery. None of them
were known outlaws, and no one suspected their in-
volvement. The operation, for all practical purposes,
was foolproof.

Subsequently, Starbuck discovered that Yeager had
not been entirely forthcoming. Over the next two
days, while they waited for the gang to assemble, he
listened more than he talked. From snatches of conversation between Yeager and Reeves, he slowly became aware that the operation was both complex and
skillfully organized. Altogether, there were apparently
a dozen or more gang members. Some lived in town
and others worked claims along Alder Gulch. Yet they
were rotated from job to job, and only five or six men
took part in any one holdup. As a result, their periodic

absences went unnoticed, and thereby the risk of exposure was reduced. The same men were never used on two jobs running.

The greater revelation, however, had to do with the upcoming holdup. In discussions of the job, it became abundantly clear that Yeager had inside information. He already knew the value of the express shipment, and he was certain it would depart Virginia City on the morning stage. The clincher came when he told them the strongbox would be secreted beneath the floorboards of the coach. While he made no mention of an informant, the conclusion was all too obvious. There was a Judas working for the stageline.

The gang members themselves were no great surprise. To a man, they were cold and callous, and placed little or no value on human life. They joked openly about express guards who had put up a fight and died in the effort. Yet, for all their grisly humor, they treated Starbuck with grudging respect. The story of his shootout with Pete Johnson had made the rounds, and none of them doubted his coolness under fire. Still, he was an unknown quantity as a robber, which caused them to reserve judgment. His test would come on the stage road to Dillon.

Starbuck was under no illusions. Today, as they rode higher into the mountains, he knew he would have but one chance to prove himself. Steady nerves and teamwork were attributes demanded of every member of the gang. A new recruit who appeared shaky—or too much of a lone wolf—was a risk no one could afford; his first job would be his last. Starbuck understood the danger and accepted it without qualms. He had every intention of pulling his own weight.

The holdup went off without a hitch. Yeager selected a sharp switchback on an uphill grade. Then he posted two men on either side of the road, with himself to the front and Reeves to the rear. An hour or so later, the stagecoach slowly rounded the curve. On the grade, the driver was forced to hold his horses to a walk, with no chance for a sudden burst of speed. Yeager simply stepped into the road while the others rose from hiding and covered the stage. All of them were masked, brandishing their weapons in a threatening manner, and Yeager's commands were obeyed without hesitation. The express guard dropped his shotgun, and the passengers obligingly tore up the floorboards and tossed out the strongbox. From start to finish, the robbery took less than ten minutes. Then the stage was allowed to proceed on its way.

The strongbox was carried into the woods. There Yeager blew off the lock with his pistol. The contents were an equal mix of bullion, gold dust, and bags of coins. The value, listed on an enclosed manifest, was fifty-six thousand dollars. While the men laughed and clowned, Yeager divvied the loot into separate piles. Reeves brought his own horse and Yeager's horse forward, and one pile went into their saddlebags. The other pile, amounting to some five thousand dollars per man, was divided among the gang members. Then they mounted and scattered to the winds.

Yeager asked Starbuck to wait behind. He left Reeves loading the saddlebags and walked Starbuck back to the road. His face was twisted in a possum grin.

"Well, what d'you think? Was I lyin' or not?"

"Hell, no!" Starbuck laughed. "Easiest money I ever made in my life."

"Figgered you wouldn't have no complaint."

"No complaint," Starbuck agreed. "But I got a question."

"What's on your mind?"

"How come you take half?" Starbuck inquired easily. "You never told me it worked that way."

Yeager gave him a dirty look. "It don't pay to get greedy."

"A man's entitled to ask."

"I plan the job and it's me that takes most of the risks! On top of that, I guarantee every time you ride you'll get a payday. Which ain't exactly nothin' to sniff at! So let's just say it all evens out in the end."

"I wasn't bellyachin' . . . just curious."

"Now you know." Yeager studied the ground a moment, then glanced up. "You handled yourself real good, Lee. Keep your nose clean and stay out of trouble. I'll be in touch before long."

"Any idea how long?"

"Don't get antsy," Yeager ordered. "When I've got a payday lined up, you'll hear about it. Understand?"

"Whatever you say, Frank."

Starbuck waved and swung aboard his horse. He reined about and rode toward Virginia City. The thought occurred that he could have killed Yeager just now and reported the case closed. Yet he knew that would have been only a half-truth. Frank Yeager was not the man he'd been hired to kill.

Over the last four days Starbuck had studied the gang leader closely. Yeager possessed a certain cunning, and he was an excellent tactician when it came to pulling a holdup. But he was no mental giant, hardly a thinker. Nor had he displayed the flair for organization and planning that were the hallmarks of the operation. He was a field commander, nothing more.

Simple deduction led to an obvious conclusion. Somehow, in a way not yet revealed, the entire operation was directed by a mastermind. The robbers themselves were little more than puppets; someone in the background pulled the strings. One intriguing possibility was that the Judas and the mastermind might be the same man. Only time and deeper investigation would tell. But of one thing there was no longer a shred of doubt. Frank Yeager was merely the gang leader. He was not the ringleader.

And that was the man Starbuck had been hired to kill.

Chapter Nine

Outside Virginia City, Starbuck turned north. He skirted the town until he hit the rutted wagon trail. Then he rode west toward Rattlesnake Creek.

Earlier, upon parting company with Yeager, he'd been undecided as to his next move. He was convinced Yeager took orders from whoever masterminded the robberies. There was also reason to believe that inside information was being passed along to the gang. It followed, then, that there was a pipeline into either the express office or the stageline company. The Judas was someone with access to confidential shipment schedules, highly restricted information. All of which put a whole new complexion on the problem.

Starbuck could no longer afford to trust anyone. Topping the list were the men who had hired him. Munro Salisbury, president of the stageline, had direct knowledge of the express shipments. John Duggan, who headed the mining association, was also privy to inside matters. It seemed unlikely that either man was directly implicated in the holdups. Yet, however improbable, it was nonetheless a factor that merited consideration. The greater likelihood was that the Judas enjoyed the confidence of one or both of the men. So anything they knew was very probably known by the Judas. That being the case, the option of contacting either Salisbury or Duggan was foreclosed. To do so would risk blowing his cover.

Still, Starbuck desperately needed a lead. His suspicions were valueless without hard evidence. He somehow had to unearth the identity of the mastermind and ringleader, not to mention the Judas. But he couldn't confide in Salisbury or Duggan, nor could he question them as to likely suspects. By process of elimination, that left only Frank Yeager.

Several things were apparent. Foremost was that Yeager's half of the loot would somehow be split with the ringleader. Unless Starbuck missed his guess, the division would occur fairly rapidly. There was little honor among thieves, and Yeager would not be entrusted with the haul for any length of time. The premise seemed solid, and from it evolved two very distinct possibilities. The ringleader would appear at Yeager's ranch and collect his share of the spoils. Or, barring that, Yeager would deliver the split to someone in Virginia City. One way or the other, an exchange was inevitable.

In Starbuck's view, it boiled down to a matter of risk. The ringleader would place himself in greater jeopardy by traveling to Yeager's ranch. Aside from the risk of being seen, it would immediately establish a connection. The wiser choice would be to effect the exchange in Virginia City. For one thing, Yeager's appearance in town would draw little attention. For another, the teeming crowds and street activity offered a better chance of secrecy. Yeager could move about at will and pick his time. No one would suspect he was there to make a payoff.

For all that, Starbuck was still determined to hedge his bet. He'd learned long ago that trying to outguess a crook was a sticky proposition. The only certainty was that the exchange would take place at night. Anyone cunning enough to organize the robberies would not hazard a payoff in broad daylight. Whether at Yeager's ranch or in Virginia City, the meeting would occur under the cloak of darkness. So there was only one logical spot to set up a surveillance. And that spot was Rattlesnake Creek.

Late that afternoon, Starbuck dismounted in a grove of trees. To the west, the sun was dipping lower behind the mountains. He tied his horse and walked forward to the creek. Yeager's house was some distance beyond the far bank, but easily visible. He took a position screened by the treeline and lit a cigarette. Then he settled down to wait.

Everything appeared in order. Yeager and Reeves, much as he'd expected, had taken a shortcut through the mountains. Their horses were unsaddled and standing hipshot in the corral. By rough estimate, he calculated they had ridden into the ranch some two hours ago. A tendril of smoke drifted from the chimney, and he caught the scent of coffee on an upwind breeze. He imagined they were eating supper about now, and his stomach rumbled in protest. The detective business, he told himself wryly, was a tough way to make a living. Outlaws had all the best of it . . . till the end.

Starbuck's wait ended three cigarettes later. As dusk settled over the land Yeager emerged from the house. His saddlebags were thrown over his shoulder, and the weight was sufficient to make him list. There seemed little doubt the pockets were stuffed with bullion and gold dust. He walked swiftly to the corral and draped the saddlebags over the top rail. Then he caught up his horse and snubbed him near the gate. He began saddling.

Easing away from the creek, Starbuck hurried through the trees. His hunch had panned out; Yeager was headed for Virginia City and a payoff. Yet Starbuck knew an even larger gamble was about to commence. To trail Yeager into town—in the dark— would require that he stick too close for comfort. Even if Yeager didn't spot him, the sound of hoofbeats from behind would betray his presence. Either way, it would alert Yeager and spoil the game. So he had no choice but to ride ahead and take up watch on the outskirts of town. He was betting Yeager would stick to the wagon road.

He mounted and galloped hell-for-leather toward Virginia City.

The night was dark as pitch. Starbuck stood in the shadows of a whorehouse at the west end of Wallace Street. The red-light district was swarming with miners, every crib and bagnio turning them away at the doors. No one even glanced in his direction.

Starbuck judged it to be somewhere around eleven o'clock. He'd been waiting nearly two hours, and still no sign of Yeager. While he'd pushed his horse, he hadn't thought Yeager would poke along. Unless the gang leader showed soon, it would mean he had circled and entered town somewhere else. Or worse, that his destination was not Virginia City after all. A sinking feeling crept over Starbuck as he considered the thought.

Then, suddenly, he stiffened and edged deeper into the shadows. Yeager rode past at a walk, slumped slouch-shouldered in the saddle. Starbuck tugged his hat low and joined the stream of miners on the boardwalk. He stayed a good twenty paces behind, following slowly as Yeager moved toward the center of town. At the next corner, Yeager turned south on Van Buren. Starbuck kept to the north side of Wallace and stopped at the corner. He saw Yeager rein into an alleyway.

Crossing the street, Starbuck hurried to the alley. He eased his head around the corner of a building and watched as Yeager rode halfway down the block. There the gang leader halted at the intersection of an alleyway which ran in the opposite direction. He took a long look around, then dismounted and moved across the intersection on foot. He hitched his horse to the banister of a stair landing and quickly unfastened his saddle bags. With the saddlebags thrown over his shoulder, he climbed the stairs to a second-floor landing. He stopped before a door and knocked. Several moments passed before the door opened in a flood of light. He stepped inside.

Starbuck's pulse skipped a beat. The distant alley was the one in which he'd killed Pete Johnson. It flanked the Gem Theater and emerged onto Wallace Street, the town's main thoroughfare. More to the point, Lola had told him that Omar Stimson, the theater owner, had an office on the second floor. Frank Yeager had just climbed the stairs to the Gem's rear entrance.

Whirling around, Starbuck sprinted back to the corner. He turned onto Wallace Street and rushed along the boardwalk. He bulled through the throngs of miners, roughly shoving and jostling as he moved down the block. When he pulled up outside the Gem, no more than thirty seconds had passed since he'd observed Yeager mount the stairs. He pushed through the bat-wing doors and halted.

The barroom was packed with a boisterous crowd. His gaze swept the room, then abruptly stopped. He saw Omar Stimson standing behind several miners at one of the faro layouts. The play was heavy, and the Gem's owner seemed to have his eye on the dealer. As Starbuck watched, a bouncer threaded his way through the men ganged around the table. Tapping Stimson on the shoulder, he whispered something under his breath and jerked a thumb upstairs. Stimson asked a question, and the bouncer bobbed his head. After a moment, one eye still on the faro game, Stimson turned away. The bouncer swiftly cleared a path.

Starbuck held his place by the door. He lit a cigarette, gazing over the flare of the match. Stimson, preceded by the bouncer, crossed the room and went up the stairs to the second floor. On the upper landing, they entered a hallway and walked toward the rear of the building. Starbuck snuffed the match and took a long, thoughtful drag.

All of it fitted and everything he'd seen made sense. Yet he was struck by a sudden doubt. Some visceral instinct told him things were not as they appeared.

Omar Stimson wasn't the man he'd been hired to kill.

Starbuck sat concealed behind a trash heap. Across from him was Yeager's horse and the stairway leading to the Gem's rear entrance. Some fifteen minutes had elapsed since he'd walked from the theater and found himself a vantage point in the alley. He waited with the patience of a hunter stalking dangerous game.

His conviction was stronger now. What began as a swift-felt impulse had been buttressed by hard-won experience. After seven years as a detective, he had gained considerable insight into the mentality of criminals. One of the prime lessons he'd learned had to do with the inner workings of the underworld. There was a certain code which governed any criminal enterprise. The more complex the operation, the more rigid the system became; where big money was involved, the rules were all but carved in stone. The code was formulated by the underworld hierarchy, and it was enforced with ruthless savagery. No one broke the rules and lived.

So far, the chain of command had followed a standard pattern. Frank Yeager recruited men into the gang and led them in the actual holdups. Yet he op-

erated under the sanction of someone at a higher level,
and he was accountable for every job. Clearly, the
man he reported to was Omar Stimson, the vice czar
of Virginia City. In turn, Stimson answered to someone still higher. A percentage of all criminal activity—
whether vice or stage robbery—was funneled to a
man at the top. An overlord whose word was law in
any underworld enterprise. A man with political clout.

In Starbuck's experience, vice and politics were in-
separable. Without political protection, no vice czar
could exert control over the diverse elements within
the underworld. He'd found it to be true in other mining camps, such as Tombstone and Deadwood. On
another assignment, which took him to San Francisco,
the trail had led from train robbers to a vice boss to
a political kingpin. Even in Denver, his own town, a
thug named Lou Blomger controlled vice and crime
through dominance of the political apparatus. Never
before had he encountered an exception. Wherever he
traveled, he found politics and vice to be the original
strange bedfellows. Virginia City would prove no different.

Hidden behind the trash heap, Starbuck considered
the knotty question of how to proceed. Frank Yeager
was plainly an underling, low man on the totem pole.
He could easily be captured and made to talk.
Charged with robbery and murder, he would gladly
spill his guts to avoid the hangman's noose. That
would implicate Stimson and thereby place him on
the road to the gallows. Still, there was a vast difference between the two men. A stage robber was ex-

pendable, merely a pawn to be sacrificed. A vice czar
was virtually immune to prosecution.

Stimson was a dominant force in the underworld.
By extension, that made him a key member of the
local power structure. Should he decide to name
names, he could implicate the man—or men—who
ruled Virginia City. Therefore, even if he were taken
into custody, he would not talk. Whoever he reported
to would grant him immunity in exchange for silence.
No indictment would be handed down and he would
not stand trial. He would, instead, walk away free.

Accordingly, Starbuck saw nothing to be gained by
hasty action. The smarter move was to lie low and
play a waiting game. Yeager had led him to Stimson,
and that was by no means the end of the trail. Nor
was it the last of the payoffs. The haul from the robbery would be split once again, and this time Stimson
would make the delivery. Perhaps tonight, maybe not
until tomorrow. But Starbuck thought it would be
done without undue delay. He planned to follow
wherever Stimson led.

Shortly before midnight Yeager emerged from the
upstairs office. His saddlebags were empty, and he
came down the stairs like a man relieved of a burden.
Then he mounted his horse and rode off. Starbuck
simply hid and watched. He was resigned to a long
wait.

Not ten minutes later the door again opened. The
bouncer stepped onto the upstairs landing and peered
around the alley. He was a bruiser, heavily muscled,
with a thick neck and powerful shoulders. A bulge
underneath his suit jacket indicated he had a pistol

stuffed in the waistband of his trousers. At length, he turned and signaled the all clear. Omar Stimson moved through the door and followed him down the stairway. The vice czar was carrying a leather satchel.

Starbuck suddenly felt vindicated. The bouncer was clearly riding shotgun on the contents of the satchel. Which meant everyone involved knew the robbery had taken place and they were expecting to be paid off tonight. He waited until Stimson and the goon reached the end of the alley. When they rounded the corner onto Van Buren Street, he quit the trash heap. He tailed them at a discreet distance.

Stimson's route was an exercise in stealth. With the bouncer at his elbow, he crossed Wallace and proceeded north on Van Buren. Halfway down the block he turned sharply into an unlighted alley. From there he walked eastward and emerged on Jackson Street. Then he again swung north, moving past several darkened business establishments. Near the corner, he stopped and rapped on a door. A few moments later the door opened in a shaft of light. Stimson and the bruiser stepped inside, and the door closed behind them.

Starbuck hesitated at the mouth of the alley. Streetlamps flickered at both ends of the block, and he was wary of being spotted. Finally, satisfied there was no one about, he crossed to the east side of Jackson Street, Hugging the shadows, he darted from doorway to doorway, working his way toward the far corner. Some distance down the block, he ducked into the doorway of a hardware store and flattened himself against the wall. Almost directly opposite him was the building Stimson and the bouncer had entered. The blind was drawn, but the glow of a lamp shone from inside. On the plate-glass window was a sign done in fancy gold scrollwork. The lettering was dimly illuminated by the corner streetlight:

ALDER GULCH ASSAY COMPANY
Cyrus Skinner
President

The name meant nothing. Yet the connection, however tenuous, was immediately apparent to Starbuck. An assayer was actively involved in the gold-mining business and privy to all sorts of privileged information. Which tended to raise more questions than it answered. Was Skinner the ringleader or the Judas or the political kingpin? Or was he all three rolled into one? Then, again, perhaps he was none of those things. It was entirely possible that Stimson used him to dispose of the stolen bullion and gold dust. Still, whatever else he was, the assayer was definitely another link in the chain. A bit of investigation might very well prove him to be the last link. The Virginia City overlord.

Across the street, the door of the assay office abruptly opened. Stimson's bouncer stepped outside and swung the door shut. Starbuck had only a moment to wonder why Stimson had remained behind. Then he realized he was in an exposed position, perfectly visible. The bouncer glanced in his direction and froze.

There was nothing for it. The options were to kill

the man on the spot or attempt to run a bluff. Starbuck
hastily unbuttoned his pants and pulled out his pud.
For a moment his bladder seemed paralyzed, and he
thought it was a lost cause. Then he gritted his teeth
and strained and finally got the waterworks into operation. He doused the hardware store door with a
steamy spray that sounded wetly in the still night. A
puddle formed around his boots, and he shook his pud
once for good measure. Finished, he tucked himself
away and pretended to fumble with the buttons on his
pants.

The bouncer was watching him intently. Yet Starbuck thought his chances were improving by the moment. He was wearing a common mackinaw, and his
features were somewhat obscured in the silty glow of
the streetlamp. By acting the part, he might still pass
himself off as a drunken miner. He wobbled out of
the doorway, careful to keep his head ducked low.
Staggering along, he lurched and swayed with the
rubbery-legged gait of a man crocked to the gills. At
the corner, he walked straight into the lamppost and
rebounded with a muttered curse. A quick glance confirmed that the bouncer was watchful but apparently
not alarmed. Starbuck rounded the corner and went
weaving down the street.

The immediate danger had passed. Whether or not
he'd fooled the bouncer completely remained to be
seen. Tomorrow he would put it to the test and find
out. But for now he had a more pressing problem. A
question that still echoed through his mind.

Who—and what—was Cyrus Skinner?

Chapter Ten

Starbuck went about his usual routine the next day. He thought it important that everything appear normal. Another unremarkable day in the life of Lee Hall.

Yet his nerves were raw with tension. When he awakened, he felt oddly unsure about what lay ahead. He mentally reviewed the events of last night while he shaved. There was every chance he would be asked questions; his answers would have to be both believable and convincing. Otherwise, today might be his last day in the guise of Lee Hall.

His concern centered on two seemingly unrelated matters. The first had to do with his horse. Upon arriving in town the previous evening, he'd gone straightaway to the livery stable near Chinatown. He had ridden hard, and he figured he was at least a half hour ahead of Frank Yeager. At the livery, he had rented a stall and insisted on looking after the horse himself. That gave him an opportunity to ditch the sacks of gold dust and coins stowed in his saddlebags. He scooped away straw and manure and dug a hole in the floor of the stall. Then he buried the gold, certain that no one would poke around beneath a pile of horse apples. After tending to the horse, he'd crossed town and taken up his post outside the whorehouse. There was only one flaw in his actions to that point. Anyone who cared to check could easily establish the time he'd arrived in town. He would have to be prepared for questions.

His second concern was by far the more troublesome. The close call last night with Stimson's bouncer still weighed heavily. He thought he'd pulled it off; the drunken-miner act was one of his more memorable performances. But he'd learned long ago never to take anything for granted. It was entirely possible the bouncer had recognized him. Apparently, after delivering the satchel, Stimson had dismissed the man and stayed behind for a private talk with Cyrus Skinner. Whether or not the bouncer had returned and informed Stimpson of the incident was the key question. In retrospect, Starbuck concluded he must assume it had happened in just that manner. False confidence, particularly at this juncture, was a pitfall he could ill afford. Better to put it to the test and determine where he stood. Tonight he would beard Stimson at the theater watchful for any telltale signs of hostility. A bold front might very well turn the trick.

In the meantime, there was the matter of Cyrus Skinner. Starbuck was somewhat at a loss as to where he should start. The assayer was a complete cipher, an unknown quantity. His association with Stimson appeared anything but legitimate; their clandestine meeting directly linked him to the stage holdups. Yet his overall role presented a whole grab bag of possibilities. He might be anything from a fence for the stolen gold to the political kingpin of Virginia City.

An investigation, however, would prove a tricky proposition. Overt snooping would pose the hazard of alarming both Stimson and Skinner. So the questions would have to be framed in a casual manner and directed to people who had no dealings with either man. That greatly limited the scope of the investigation and bothered Starbuck more than he cared to admit. Still, he saw no alternative to discreet inquiry. He was too close to risk blowing the case.

Starbuck emerged from the hotel at noontime. As was his custom, he went directly to a café across the street. There he wolfed down a breakfast of beefsteak and eggs and sourdough biscuits. He topped off the meal with a cup of coffee strong enough to grow hair and left a four-bit tip. Outside, with a toothpick stuck in his mouth, he stood for a while basking in the sun. Then he strolled upstreet at a leisurely pace.

The afternoon was spent drifting from saloon to saloon. Starbuck shot a few games of pool and let himself be conned into a small-stakes poker game. The sporting crowd was out and about, and they greeted him as one of the fraternity. Everywhere he went he bought drinks for others, while he himself nursed a schooner of beer. His conviviality, along with the free drinks, assured him of company at every stop. He talked with bartenders and gamblers, thimbleriggers and shills, and a seemingly endless parade of saloon girls. One way or another, he steered the conversation onto gold and the looming prospect of quartz mining. From there, he worked the talk around to promising claims and the latest assay reports. A leading question sometimes brought the name of Cyrus Skinner into the discussion. Then he listened a lot, pretending off-hand interest and bored curiosity. By the end of the day, he'd pumped the sporting crowd for all they knew. It wasn't much.

Cyrus Skinner was an old-timer in Virginia City. He'd opened a one-man assay office shortly after gold was discovered along Alder Gulch. As the camp mushroomed into a boomtown his business had prospered and grown, until now he pretty much had a corner on the assay market. He was a mainstay in the local Democratic party, though he'd never held office or achieved prominence in the political arena. Widely respected, he was known as a man of character and scrupulous honesty. He took an occasional drink but shunned the gambling dens and apparently steered clear of the town's parlor houses. According to the sporting crowd, he was a rabid civic booster and a man with no known vices. Which made him square as a cube.

Starbuck retired to his hotel room shortly after sundown. He sprawled out on the bed and slowly digested all he'd learned. While none of it was revealing, the sum and substance sparked his cynicism. Any man with no known vices was, in his view, automatically suspect. A veneer of morality all too often masked oddments of an unwholesome nature. Based on what he had seen last night, that seemed very much the case with Cyrus Skinner. But he still had no cold, hard facts, no proof. Nor had he the slightest notion of where to look.

With the onset of darkness, he rose and lighted a lamp. Tomorrow, even though it was a risk he preferred to avoid, he would kick over one last stone. He had only a vague hope that it would uncover anything new and startling about the mysterious assayer. Tonight he would tackle another, and equally unsettling, problem. The matter of Omar Stimson and his eagle-eyed bouncer.

Starbuck began washing up for supper. As he soaped his hands his gaze was attracted to his warbag. He always left it on the floor beside the washstand, and he always left the clasps unfastened. He saw now that the clasps were fastened and the warbag itself had been moved slightly. The discovery at once angered him and sent a chill along his backbone. He knew exactly what it meant.

Someone had searched his room.

Whatever he'd expected, Starbuck's reception at the Gem was something of a shock. He no sooner bellied up to the bar than Omar Stimson appeared at his elbow. The theater owner greeted him warmly and ordered a drink on the house.

"Been out of town?" Stimson inquired genially. "I missed you the last few days."

Starbuck thought it a crafty ploy. The question revealed nothing and it still opened up a can of worms. He had no idea where it would lead, but he decided to play along.

"I'm surprised you even knew I was gone."

"You're a regular now, Lee! I always look after a good customer."

"Well, like I told you before—" Starbuck paused

and sipped his drink. "I got business that takes me here and there."

"Oh, I remember!" Stimson laughed. "A little of this and a little of that. Wasn't that it?"

Starbuck smiled. "I don't gather much moss."

"Some folks are wondering about that very thing."

"What d'you mean?"

"I hear Sheriff Palmer has been asking around about you."

"Why so?"

"Big excitement yesterday." Stimson fixed him with a sly look. "The morning stage to Dillon was robbed. Or hadn't you heard?"

"Somebody mentioned it," Starbuck said vaguely. "Are you trying to tell me the sheriff thinks I had a hand in that holdup?"

"You be the judge," Stimson replied with a shrug. "There's a rumor to the effect he searched your hotel room this afternoon."

"The hell you say!" Starbuck appeared dumbfounded. "Why would he do a thing like that?"

"I imagine he was looking for stolen gold."

"Kiss my dusty butt!" Starbuck said hotly. "Wonder where he got such a damnfool notion?"

"Word's around you got yourself a horse."

"How'd you know that?"

"People talk," Stimson said with a bland gesture. "Someone at the livery stable mentioned you'd rented a stall. When Palmer got wind of it, he went over and checked out the horse."

"What in tarnation for?"

"Evidently the sheriff has got you pegged as a bad

character. If the stage driver could identify your horse, then you'd be up a creek. See what I mean?"

"Not a chance!" Starbuck crowed. "Goddamn horse's own mother wouldn't recognize him!"

"Glad to hear it." Stimson was silent a moment, thoughtful. "One other thing you ought to consider."

"Oh?"

"The hostler said you brought your horse in a little before nine last night. In case you're asked, you better be able to account for your whereabouts."

"Simplest thing on earth!" Starbuck said boldly. "I rode in yesterday afternoon and stopped at one of the cathouses. Always take my time when I go to get my log sapped. So it was late before I made it down to the livery."

"Looks like you're in the clear, then."

"You bet your boots I am!"

Stimson chatted awhile longer, then wandered off. Starbuck wasn't quite sure what to make of the conversation. On the surface it seemed Stimson merely wanted to warn him about the sheriff. Then, again, there was an undertone of suspicion to the questions. Almost a sense of interrogation. Either way, Starbuck decided on an abrupt change of plans. Tomorrow night very well might be too late.

Tonight was the time to kick over that last stone.

A few minutes before seven, Starbuck slipped out of the Gem. He walked to the corner and crossed the street to his hotel. He went straight through the lobby and out the back door. A narrow passageway between buildings led to Jackson Street, and there he paused. He slowly inspected the street in both directions.

The town's main intersection, which he'd crossed only moments before, was clogged with the usual nighttime crowd. Jackson Street itself was dimly lighted and appeared empty. At length, satisfied he hadn't been followed, he stepped from the passageway. He hurriedly moved to the opposite side of the street and cut into the alley. A quick walk brought him to Van Buren, and there he turned north. George Hoyt's office was a few doors up the block.

On his previous visit Starbuck had found the lawyer working late. He was banking on that being the case tonight. Otherwise, he would have to ask directions to Hoyt's home, and that would compound an already dicey situation. His luck held. A beam of light filtered through the plate-glass window. He strode rapidly to the door and ducked inside.

George Hoyt looked up from his desk. His expression was one of surprise and mild curiosity. Then, still silent, he watched Starbuck lock the door and pull the blind. The disguise was different, but Starbuck's furtive manner triggered a memory of their last meeting. Hoyt suddenly made the connection, and his face went slack with fear.

"You!"

"Nobody else." Starbuck moved forward and took a chair. "Figured it was time we had ourselves another talk!"

"But I—" Hoyt stammered. "I kept my word! I spoke to no one about you or our conversation!"

"Never doubted it," Starbuck assured him. "That's not why I'm here."

"What do you want, then?"

"We're going to make a swap. You come clean and provide me with certain information. In return, I'll keep you out of prison."

"Prison!" Hoyt shook his head dumbly. "What are you talking about?"

"Cyrus Skinner."

Hoyt's mouth popped open and he sat transfixed. His face went chalky, and behind the wire-rimmed glasses a pinpoint of terror surfaced in his eyes. When at last he spoke, his voice had an unusual timbre.

"I have nothing to say . . . nothing."

"Yeah, you do," Starbuck said tightly. "I'll spell it out for you. Frank Yeager and Omar Stimson are going to hang for murder. Skinner will probably get a life sentence. You're just small fry, but you're still an accessory before the fact. So you're looking at twenty, maybe thirty years."

"Who are you?"

"U.S. deputy marshal," Starbuck said without expression. "I was sent here to get the stage robbers. One thing led to another, and I kept turning up more names. All I need to make a case are a few more details, and that's your way out. You come clean, and I guarantee you won't serve a day."

"I don't believe you," Hoyt said, his face careworn. "If you know so much, why do you need me?"

"Corroboration." Starbuck smiled crookedly. "I infiltrated Yeager's gang and helped him rob the stage yesterday. Then I trailed him to Stimson, and Stimson led me to Skinner. You turn state's evidence—corroborate my story—and you're off the hook. Otherwise, you win yourself a striped suit."

There was a stretch of deadened silence. Hoyt seemed caught up in a moment of indecision, and his eyes drifted away. Then he pursed his lips in a forlorn expression.

"What do you want to know?"

"Tell me about Skinner." Starbuck regarded him evenly. "I've already got the goods on Yeager and Stimson."

"Cyrus Skinner," Hoyt said hollowly, "controls the county political machine. He purposely stays out of the limelight, but he's the power behind the throne. No one gets into public office without his stamp of approval."

"Which includes you?"

"Yes." Hoyt was unable to meet his gaze. "Skinner handpicked me for county prosecutor. As an added inducement, he promised to back me for the legislature in next year's election. I agreed to turn a blind eye to the robberies and other irregularities."

"Such as?"

"Graft and corruption. Skinner uses Omar Stimson as a front man. All the vice operations pay protection money, and it ends up in Skinner's pocket."

"How about Sheriff Palmer?" Starbuck persisted. "Is he Skinner's man, too?"

"Palmer's the exception," Hoyt said softly. "He's a political maverick, an independent. He campaigned on his own ticket and beat Skinner's candidate three to one."

"Why hasn't he gone after Skinner?"

"Why would he?" Hoyt responded. "Very few people even know that Skinner's the kingpin. He operates through others and keeps himself insulated from the dirty work."

"What about the robbers Palmer caught? The ones you tried and hanged. Were they part of Yeager's gang?"

Hoyt gave him a dull stare. "Those men were just garden-variety bandits. So far as I know, Palmer doesn't suspect an organized gang. He certainly doesn't suspect Yeager! No one does."

"Palmer's no dimdot," Starbuck said doubtfully. "Are you saying he doesn't suspect there's a Judas working for the stage company?"

"Judas?"

"An inside man," Starbuck elaborated. "Someone who supplies advance information on the gold shipments."

"Good Lord!" Hoyt's mouth froze in a silent oval. "I always wondered how Yeager picked the right stages!"

"You mean nobody ever said anything to you about an inside man?"

"Not a word," Hoyt said with a hangdog look. "But then, of course, I never asked. I didn't want to know the details, especially beforehand. Too many express guards were being killed."

Starbuck read no guile in his face. "All right, we'll let that pass. What about Doc Carver? How'd he get involved?"

"He wasn't involved," Hoyt remarked. "He was just an innocent bystander."

"Then how come he took off running?"

"He had no choice," Hoyt said miserably. "His daughter—Alice—learned something she wasn't supposed to know."

"What was that . . . just exactly?"

"I have no idea." Hoyt swallowed and his Adam's apple bobbed. "Skinner refused to discuss it with me."

"Did Skinner know you were sweet on the Carver girl?"

"Oh, yes." A look of anguish came into Hoyt's eyes. "He knew how I felt. He knew it all along."

"Was Skinner the one who murdered her?"

"She—" Hoyt faltered, his voice barely audible. "Alice wasn't killed."

"She's alive!" Starbuck was genuinely astounded. "The Carver girl's alive?"

"Alice and her father—"

The window exploded and a trash can struck the floor in a shower of glass. Starbuck reacted on sheer instinct and threw himself backward in his chair. He crashed into the wall, pulling his Colt as the chair collapsed and he toppled to the floor. Hoyt jackknifed to his feet and gaped at two men dimly visible through the shattered window. Then the men opened fire with sawed-off shotguns; three quick blasts hammered Hoyt into the rear wall. The fourth blast ripped away the top of his head, and his knees buckled. He slumped forward beneath a mist of brains and gore.

Starbuck levered himself up on one arm before the men could reload. He sighted on the shadowy figures and thumbed off a hurried snap shot. One of the men screamed and dropped his scattergun. Starbuck triggered another shot and then realized he was firing at an empty window. The men were gone, and in the sudden stillness he heard pounding footsteps on the boardwalk. He stood, moved swiftly to the window, and took a cautious look outside. He saw the men turn the corner of a building and disappear into the alley. Muttering to himself, he cursed the darkness and his own shooting. The man he'd hit wasn't wounded seriously, for they were both running at top speed. He sensed there was nothing to be gained by chasing after them.

A look around confirmed what he already knew. George Hoyt was dead, and with him had died any hope of a quick break in the case. Worse, the killing meant that Stimson had not been fooled. Someone had shadowed Starbuck tonight and trailed him to the lawyer's office. The masquerade was over, and he no longer needed a disguise.

His cover was blown.

Chapter Eleven

Starbuck waited near the door. A crowd of morbid onlookers was gathered outside the shattered window. To the rear of the office, Sheriff Palmer and a deputy were inspecting the corpse. Their features were grim, their voices a low murmur.

In the aftermath of the shooting, several miners had collected on the boardwalk. Gunfire tended to draw spectators, and word of the killing quickly spread uptown. Starbuck had sent a man to fetch the sheriff and then kept the crowd at a distance. The shotgun and a splotch of blood on the boardwalk were his alibi. He'd thought it prudent to preserve the evidence.

Henry Palmer had arrived shortly thereafter. Starbuck, still in the guise of Lee Hall, had related the details of the killing. But he had refused to explain his presence in the lawyer's office. Only in private, he insisted, would he elaborate further. A quick look around convinced the sheriff that Starbuck had not participated in the murder. The fresh blood trail outside, along with the shotgun, indicated Starbuck had wounded one of the assassins. The condition of the deceased, riddled with four loads of buckshot, verified that two men had taken part in the shooting. Palmer had agreed to withhold judgment, pending a full explanation.

Under other circumstances, Starbuck would have taken matters into his own hands. Cyrus Skinner was clearly the man he'd been hired to kill. Yet he realized that any attempt to call Skinner out would accomplish nothing. There was no hard evidence, and the assayer would simply refuse to fight. No assassin, Starbuck could hardly kill Skinner in cold blood. He always gave a hunted man a chance, however slight. The fact that he'd blown his cover further complicated the situation. So the alternative, at least for the moment, was to work through the law. He saw it as the only way to build a solid case.

Palmer's examination took less than a half hour. He dispatched someone with a message for the undertaker and left his deputy to guard the murder scene. Once the body was removed, he ordered that the window be boarded up and the door locked. Then, motioning to Starbuck, he led the way outside. The crowd parted, and they walked toward Wallace Street. Neither man spoke.

All the way across town Starbuck weighed various options. He wondered how little he could tell Palmer and still obtain the lawman's cooperation. The fly in the ointment was Cyrus Skinner. He had only circumstantial evidence, and he needed hard-and-fast proof before he could act. Then there was the additional factor of the Judas. He still had no positive identification, and he'd lost all chance of operating undercover. So it was vital that the sheriff commence an immediate investigation. In the end, he decided to tell Palmer everything.

A short while later they entered the sheriff's office. The furnishings were sparse, with a single battered desk and several wooden armchairs. Off the main room, several barred cells were visible along a corridor. To all appearances, there were no prisoners in the lockup and they had the place to themselves. Palmer hooked his hat on a wall peg and circled around the desk. He waved Starbuck to a chair.

"Let's get down to cases." He dropped into a swivel chair, elbows on the desk. "What was your business with George Hoyt?"

Starbuck lit a cigarette, exhaled smoke. "It's a long story, and no need to cover the same ground twice. Why don't I start at the beginning?"

"Start anywhere you please."

"Well, first off, I'm not Lee Hall. The name's Luke Starbuck. I'm a private detective, operating out of Denver."

"I assume you can prove that?"

"Check with Munro Salisbury and John Duggan. They hired me, and they'll vouch for the fact that I've been working undercover."

"If you are Starbuck"—Palmer fixed him with a stern look—"you've got a rep as a mankiller. Were you sent here to put somebody away?"

"I was hired to bust up a gang of stage robbers."

"That doesn't answer my question."

Starbuck hesitated, chose his words with care. "I've never killed a man unless he was trying to kill me."

"All right, skip it for now." Palmer's frown deepened. "What's this about a gang of robbers?"

Starbuck briefly recounted the details of his assignment. He covered the salient points leading to his infiltration of Yeager's gang. Then he went on to relate how he'd tied both Stimson and Skinner to the robbery ring. He finished by repeating everything George Hoyt had told him.

"That's pretty much the story," he concluded. "Hoyt's confession nailed it down tight."

Palmer merely listened, coldly silent, eyeing him with a mixture of dismay and surprise. He drummed the desktop with his fingers, digesting what he'd heard. Then he leaned back in the creaky swivel chair.

"If it's true, that would mean Skinner rigged Alice Carver's death. What was the purpose?"

"Hoyt was just about to tell me when the shooting started. So I never found out."

"What would it have to do with the stage robberies?"

"Good question," Starbuck admitted. "I frankly don't know."

"Maybe Hoyt was feeding you a line."

"How so?"

"Somebody with a score to settle was out to get him. They tried once before and got the Carver girl instead. Sounds to me like he was trying to mislead you—throw you off the track."

"Why would he invent a story about the girl?"

"Beats me." Palmer massaged his jaw, considering. "But there's one thing I can tell you for a fact—Alice Carver is dead!"

"What makes you so certain?"

"I saw it myself! Hoyt sent for me the night she was killed. Her dress was covered with blood and she was cold as a mackerel. No maybe about it!"

"Did you feel her pulse?"

"Hell, no!" Palmer said sharply. "I know a corpse when I see one!"

"Hoyt told me it happened late at night. In the dark, it'd be easy to fake something like that . . . wouldn't it?"

A strange light came into Palmer's eyes. "I still don't buy it. We buried her the very next day! I was standing right there when they put her in the grave."

"Where was her father?"

"He vamoosed sometime during the night."

"Gets curiouser and curiouser, don't it?"

Palmer was silent for a time. At last, as though to underscore the question, he looked Starback squarely in the eye. "What are you after? Let's quit beating around the bush and get to it."

Starbuck flicked an ash off his cigarette. "I want to exhume the Carver girl's coffin."

"Dig her up?" Palmer's expression turned to blank astonishment. "Why, for Chrissake?"

"A couple of reasons," Starbuck said with dungeon calm. "If the coffin's empty—or there's someone else in it—that means Hoyt was telling the truth. In other words, somebody went to a lot of trouble to make the girl's death believable. I intend to find out why."

"What's the other reason?"

"If the murder was a fake, then it substantiates everything Hoyt told me about Skinner. Wouldn't you agree?"

"Not necessarily." Palmer steepled his fingers, peered across the desk. "We'd still have only Hoyt's word that Skinner was behind it. And a dead man's word—especially secondhand—isn't admissible in court."

Starbuck's mouth curled. "You seem to forget the daisy chain I mentioned. Yeager to Stimson to Skinner. All in one night—the night of the robbery."

"Still inadmissible," Palmer growled. "You're just guessing what Stimson had in that satchel. You couldn't swear to it under oath."

"You surprise me, Sheriff." Starbuck looked at him questioningly. "Hoyt led me to believe there's no love lost between you and Skinner. Maybe I heard him wrong."

Palmer brushed away the thought with a quick, impatient gesture. "We're in opposite political camps, but that's neither here nor there. So far as I know, Cyrus Skinner just dabbles in politics. He's no kingfish or power behind the throne! And I'll eat your hat if he's involved in these robberies. He's just too god-blessed straight!"

"That's the whole point," Starbuck noted. "He wears a starchy collar and acts holier than thou. Nobody would ever suspect he's behind the robbers and the vice payoffs. Not to mention the political shenanigans."

"Hard to swallow." Palmer lowered his head, tight-lipped. "Stimson's a different ball of wax. I wouldn't put anything past him! But I'll lay odds Skinner's no part of it."

"Why would Hoyt accuse an innocent man?"

"Who knows?" Palmer paused, jawline set in a scowl. "Maybe him and Stimson were splitting the vice payoffs. For that matter, they might've had you pegged as an undercover man from the start. Maybe the whole idea was to lead you to Skinner—put you on a blind trail."

"It won't wash." Starbuck's voice was firm. "I had them fooled down the line. It was business as usual—and nobody gave me a tumble."

"If you had them fooled"—Palmer's eyes burned with intensity—"then how come George Hoyt's dead? You slipped up somewhere, and probably more than once. Otherwise, he wouldn't have a quart of buckshot up his gizzard."

Their eyes locked. Starbuck gave him a straight, hard look, challenging him, and there was an awkward silence. He marked again that the sheriff was a cool customer, but nonetheless susceptible to spite and petty intolerance. At last, his expression stoic, he broke the impasse.

"What's your problem?" he asked bluntly. "Are you pissed off because I worked my own game in your bailiwick?"

"Wouldn't you be?" Palmer said with a flare of annoyance. "Even the Pinkertons make it standard practice to work with local law officers."

"Maybe that's why the Pinks lose so many men. I operate on a real simple principle, Sheriff. The fewer people who know about me, the longer I'll live."

"Say what you mean!" Palmer said crossly. "You didn't trust me enough to take me into your confidence. That's it in a nutshell, isn't it?"

"Nothing personal," Starbuck observed. "Until tonight, I had to play it close to the vest. All that changed after my talk with Hoyt."

"What's Hoyt got to do with me?"

"He gave you a clean bill of health . . . told me you're not involved with Skinner."

"How come you put so much faith in what a jackleg lawyer has to say?"

Starbuck dropped his cigarette on the floor, crushed it underfoot. "I had him by the short hairs, and Hoyt was no dummy. He saw a way to make a deal and save his own hide. So there was no reason for him to lie to me about Skinner. The truth was his only way out."

"I suppose it's possible," Palmer said without conviction. "But I'm still not entirely sold. Cyrus Skinner just don't seem like the type."

"Would you stake your reputation on it?"

"No," Palmer said grudgingly. "I wouldn't go that far."

"Then I take it you've got no objection to starting an investigation—do you?"

"You talking about Skinner?"

"And Stimson," Starbuck added. "I wounded one of his men tonight. I'd hazard a guess it was one of the bouncers at the Gem. Find the man and squeeze him, and he'll spill the beans on Stimson."

"Where does that get us?"

"It'll get Stimson indicted for the murder of the county prosecutor. That's one charge nobody will get quashed, not even Cyrus Skinner. Once Stimson's indicted, then you offer him a deal."

"Talk or hang!" Palmer nodded solemnly. "That what you had in mind?"

"On the button," Starbuck acknowledged. "I'll wager Stimson knows all there is to know about Skinner. Graft and political corruption, the vice payoffs and the stage holdups. You get him to turn songbird and it's all over but the shouting. He'll put a noose around Skinner's neck."

"How about Frank Yeager?"

"Hold off till you've got Stimson's balls in a nutcracker. Then you can suit yourself about Yeager. Let him hang or use him as a corroborating witness . . . whichever seems best."

Palmer looked on the verge of saying something but apparently changed his mind. He eyed Starbuck skeptically. "What are you planning to do?"

"I'll tell you in about an hour."

"An hour?"

"After we've dug up Alice Carver."

The Virginia City cemetery was on a hillside west of town. The graves were marked with wooden crosses and crude headstones. A sickle moon bathed the landscape in a pale, ghostly light.

Starbuck and Palmer were in shirtsleeves, their coats tossed on the ground. The night was chilly, and despite a brisk northwesterly wind their foreheads glistened with sweat. They dug silently, standing at opposite ends of the grave, already knee-deep in an open hole. Their shovels rose and fell with a methodical rhythm, flashing dully in the moonlight. A mound of earth was heaped at one side of the grave.

Some while earlier, they had left the sheriff's office by the back door. Palmer had expressed the opinion that the job would be easier done in daylight. Starbuck agreed, but he'd stressed the need for secrecy. He was determined that there be no leak of their visit to the graveyard. Whatever they found, if word of the exhumation got out it would immediately alert Cyrus Skinner. Thus far, only Palmer was aware of the disclosures made by George Hoyt, the murdered lawyer. That provided an edge they desperately needed. One that might well make or break the investigation.

Palmer grouched and complained, still not wholly convinced. But in the end, Starbuck's view had prevailed. A couple of shovels were collected from the jail toolshed, and they trudged off toward the cemetery. No one saw them leave town.

An hour or so had passed, and they were now hip-deep in the grave. Starbuck's shovel suddenly struck something solid, and they both paused. Then he jabbed lightly with the shovel, and a wooden *clunk* echoed from the hole. Gingerly, they began scooping out the last few inches of dirt. The top of a pine coffin slowly became visible in the dim light. After widening the hole around the sides, they stopped and leaned on their shovels. Starbuck ducked his chin at the coffin.

"Who does the honors?"

"Be my guest."

Palmer scambled out to level ground. He dusted himself off, then went to one knee beside the grave. Starbuck found footholds on either side of the hole and set himself with his back to the headstone. Then he wedged his shovel under the coffin lid and pried upward. The rusty nails protested, loosening with the screech of metal embedded deeply into wood. He worked the tip of the shovel all the way around, levering with the handle until he'd sprung the last of the nails. The lid popped free of the coffin.

Stooping down, Starbuck grasped the lid and swung it aside. He fished a match out of his vest pocket and struck it, cupping the flame in both hands. Palmer leaned into the grave as he opened his hands in a flare of light. The coffin was empty.

Starbuck doused the match and hoisted himself out of the hole. Palmer was slack-jawed, still on one knee, staring downward with stunned disbelief. A moment passed, then he stood and glanced at Starbuck with a baffled look. His face was pinched in an oxlike expression.

"I guess that makes me the prize sucker of all time."

"Forget it," Starbuck said with grim satisfaction. "I wasn't sure myself till I struck that match."

"Dirty bastards!" Palmer cursed furiously. "Half the town must have been in on it!"

"I'd tend to doubt it," Starbuck said quietly. "Outside of Skinner and his bunch, all they needed was the undertaker. Somebody probably put a gun in his ear and gave him the word. So long as it wasn't his own funeral, why should he care?"

"He'll damn sure care when I get through with him!"

"Don't go off half-cocked," Starbuck cautioned.

"Before you kick up too much dust, there's one last thing I want you to look into."

"What's that?"

"The Judas," Starbuck replied levelly. "Find him and you'll have an even stronger case against Skinner."

Palmer uttered a noncommittal grunt. "Tell you the truth, all this Judas business sounds like a pipe dream to me."

"No," Starbuck corrected him, "there's got to be an inside man. The holdups are too slick for it to work any other way. The case won't be closed till we nail him to the wall."

"Easy for you to say," Palmer grumbled. "Where would you suggest I look?"

"Omar Stimson," Starbuck advised. "Once he turns canary, he'll whistle any tune you name. Ask him about our Judas."

"Any more instructions?"

"I reckon that ought to do it."

"Then I've got a question of my own."

"Shoot."

"Now that you've looked in the coffin, what's next? You had something in mind, or we wouldn't be out robbing graves in the middle of the night."

A wintry smile lighted Starbuck's eyes. "While you're handling things here, I figured I'd tie off a loose end."

Palmer's gaze sharpened. He stared at Starbuck with the beady look of a stuffed owl. "What loose end?"

"A little lady by the name of Alice Carver."

Chapter Twelve

Starbuck traveled by stage from Virginia City. He took a roundabout route, switching from stage to train. At a whistle stop outside Butte, he finally boarded the Union Pacific eastbound. His destination was Chicago.

Once burned, Starbuck was now twice as careful. He assumed he was being watched night and day by Stimson's men. In turn, his every movement would be reported to Cyrus Skinner. He therefore took inordinate measures to guarantee he wasn't tailed. On guard constantly, he at last assured himself no one shadowed his backtrail. Only then did he discard the guise of Lee Hall and assume his own identity. He boarded the eastbound train confident his destination was unknown.

Four nights later he arrived in Chicago. Once inside the depot, he bought a newspaper and turned to the theatrical advertisements. The Buffalo Bill Combination was currently playing at Sprague's Olympic Theater. He checked his watch against the show schedule and saw that he still had time to catch the evening performance. Outside Union Station he stepped into a hansom cab and told the driver not to spare the whip.

He was anxious now for what seemed a long-overdue meeting with Alice Carver.

The ride to the Loop district was a treat in itself. Starbuck was widely traveled, but St. Louis was the largest city he'd previously visited. Framed against a full moon, the skyline of downtown Chicago was a staggering sight. The tall buildings dwarfed anything he had seen before and made Denver look like a quaint hamlet. He was particularly impressed by the brick and stone architecture, the absence of buildings constructed of wood. Then he recalled the Great Fire of '71, a holocaust that had razed three square miles and left a hundred thousand people homeless. Wood was subsequently banned as a building material in the downtown area. A new Chicago rose from the ashes, and within a year the restoration was complete. Starbuck, never easily impressed, was taken with the Windy City.

On Randolph Street, the hansom dropped him outside the theater. Show posters announced William F. Cody's appearance in an original play entitled *Buffalo Bill's Pledge*. Starbuck inquired at the box office and was directed to the stage entrance. He proceeded down a passageway between buildings and talked his way past a watchman at the rear door. Backstage was a tableau of pandemonium in motion. Frontiersmen in makeup and Indians tricked out in war paint were rushing about in a general atmosphere of confusion. A donkey, which apparently had some role in the melodrama, was braying loudly and kicking at anyone within range. To an outsider, the show business had the look of disorganized chaos.

Starbuck spotted Cody standing in the wings. The scout was attired in fringed buckskins, bleached a snowy white, and the ivory-handled Peacemakers were strapped around his waist. From beneath a broad sombrero his hair flowed over his shoulders in hot-curled waves. He turned as Starbuck spoke his name. He smelled of rosewater lotion and rye whiskey.

"Well, bless my soul!" he cackled. "Where'd you drop from, Luke?"

"Points west," Starbuck said evasively. "Just pulled in a little while ago."

"Don't tell me you came all that way to see the show!"

"Not exactly," Starbuck commented. "I'm looking for Doc Carver."

"Look no further!" Cody flung his arm in a grand gesture. "There's your man!"

Starbuck moved closer and gazed past the drawn curtains. Carver was onstage, standing near the foot-lights, with his face to the audience. He had a rifle balanced over his shoulder and he was aligning the sights through a small hand mirror. His assistant, Sally Devlin, was upstage, hands clasped behind her back and her profile turned toward him. A lighted cig-arette, trailing wisps of smoke, protruded from her lips. Below the footlights, a snare drum rolled omi-nously from the orchestra pit. Carver let the tension build a moment longer, then fired over his shoulder. The cigarette exploded in a shower of sparks and to-bacco, and the girl immediately held the shredded stub high overhead. The audience broke out in a cheering, spontaneous ovation.

Carver shamelessly milked the applause. Then, ever the consummate showman, he swiftly moved on to the next trick shot. Starbuck watched only a short time before turning back to Cody. He motioned toward the stage.

"How long does the act last?"

"Three more shots." Cody adopted a lordly stance, thumbs hooked in his gunbelt. "Doc's a great crowd pleaser! He gets them warmed up before we do the play. Always helps to have an audience in the proper mood."

"He's good, all right." Starbuck's tone was matter-of-fact. "Course, his daughter's not bad, either. Takes spunk to let yourself be shot at."

"Alice is a trouper!" Cody said effusively. "Born to the show business—a natural performer!"

"She's easy on the eyes, too."

"Very easy!" Cody lowered one eyelid in a burlesque leer. "I sometimes regret that I'm a happily married man."

"I suppose she has lots of gentlemen admirers?"

"Their number is legion, Luke! So many she has to fight them off with a switch!"

"You don't say?" Starbuck mused out loud. "The only stage women I've known were sort of fast and loose. Guess she's not that way, huh?"

"Oh—" Cody hesitated, cocked his head in a shrewd look. "All of a sudden, I detect a detective at work. Why so much interest in Alice? I thought you were here to see Doc."

"Curiosity." Starbuck spread his hands, shrugged. "Last time around, Doc introduced her to me as Sally

Devlin. I reckon it got me to wondering."

"That's just her stage name..." Cody's voice trailed off and he suddenly looked upset. "God-almighty! I recollect you told me Doc was involved in a civil suit. That wasn't so, was it? It's a divorce action, involving Alice! She's been named as a co-respondent, hasn't she?"

"Why?" Starbuck inquired calmly. "Does she play around with married men?"

"I warned Doc!" Cody fumed. "She's a wonderful girl and bright as a penny. But she's got the morals of a heathen squaw!"

"So she does play—"

Starbuck glanced past him and abruptly stopped. The stage door had opened and two men paused at the watchman's desk. One of them was Omar Stimson's bouncer, the hooligan who had spotted him on the street in Virginia City. He was vaguely aware of applause and the blare of the orchestra from the theater. He sensed the trick-shot act was ending and the Carvers would walk offstage at any moment. His gaze shifted quickly to Cody.

"Are those Peacemakers loaded?"

"Only with blanks." Cody read his expression, tensed. "What's wrong, Luke?"

"Don't look around!" Starbuck ordered. "A couple of hardcases just came through the back door. I've got reason to believe they're here to kill Alice Carver."

"Judas Priest!" Cody croaked. "What are we—"

"Shut up and listen!" Starbuck interrupted. "Do ex-actly what I say! Get out on that stage and stop the

Carver girl. Don't let her come back here! Understand?"

Cody paled. "She's already coming offstage! Her and Doc!"

"Then move—now!"

Starbuck walked toward the rear door. Behind him, he heard a muffled conversation as Cody tried to stall the Carvers. Directly ahead, the two men were moving slowly in his direction. Neither of them recognized him, for he was no longer in the guise of Lee Hall. Their eyes went instead to the wings, and Alice Carver. He halted several paces away, blocking their path.

"You boys should've stayed in Virginia City."

Too late, the men reacted to the words. Starbuck's hand was in motion even as he spoke. The Colt appeared from beneath his suit jacket and leveled at arm's length. A beat behind, the men clawed at the pistols inside their coats. Starbuck fired two rapid shots, one report blending with the other. The first slug drilled through the bouncer's breastbone and the second struck him below the left nipple. He collapsed as though his legs had been chopped off and fell spread-eagle on the floor. His sphincter voided and a bulldog pistol slipped from his hand.

The other man got off one shot. The bullet nicked Starbuck's sleeve and thudded into a stage set across the way. Starbuck brought the Colt to bear and emptied it in a blinding roar. His shots were deliberate and spaced no more than a pulsebeat apart. The heavy slugs stitched three red dots straight up the man's sternum to the base of his throat. His mouth opened in a silent scream and he vomited a hogshead of blood down his shirtfront. Then the light went out in his eyes and his knees folded like an accordion. He slumped to the floor without a sound.

Still watchful, Starbuck shucked empties and reloaded the Colt. He moved forward and checked both men, satisfying himself that they were dead. All around him the troupe of actors, frontiersmen and Indians alike, were gawking at him with looks of popeyed wonder. At last, turning away from the bodies, he directed his gaze to the stage wings. He breathed an inward sigh of relief.

Doc Carver was pressed flat against the wall. Buffalo Bill Cody had thrown the girl to the floor and covered her with his own body. She was alive and unhurt, no worse for the experience.

Starbuck promised himself she would talk.

Some hours later the backstage area had been restored to order. The police had come and gone, ruling the killings justifiable homicide. The bodies had been removed to the city morgue, and Bill Cody had led a gaggle of reporters to a nearby saloon. His recounting of the shootout had lost nothing in the telling.

On Starbuck's orders, Doc Carver and his daughter had been sequestered in the sharpshooter's dressing room. No mention of their role in the killings had been made to the police. So far as the authorities knew, the dead men had followed Starbuck to Chicago with the express purpose of assassinating him. There was no hint of the underlying scandal and the magnitude of the investigation. The police had been fobbed off with a story of stage robbers and unsolved murders.

Starbuck was now in the midst of his own interrogation. Seated across from him were Alice Carver and her father. The girl appeared in shock, and Carver's expression was somehow crestfallen. The atmosphere in the dressing room was oppressive, charged with tension.

"No more lies!" Starbuck eyed father and daughter with a steady, uncompromising gaze. "I want the truth, and I want it now. So don't try dancing me around. Talk straight and talk fast!"

Carver flushed and bobbed his head. "How did you find out . . . about Alice?"

"George Hoyt told me," Starbuck said impassively. "Just before he was murdered."

The girl began to weep, snuffling and whimpering like a hurt puppy. She pulled out a dainty handkerchief and buried her face in her hands. Carver soothed her with a shushing sound and patted her gently on the shoulder. Then he turned back to Starbuck.

"I couldn't level with you in North Platte. Surely you can understand—I had to protect Alice—at all costs! The only out I saw was to send you to Hoyt."

A stony look settled over Starbuck's features. "You and your daughter have gotten several people killed. Tonight you almost bought the farm yourselves."

"Nonsense," Carver said, a bit too quickly. "You told the police those men were after you."

"Don't play dumb!" Starbuck flared. "Skinner sent them here to kill both of you. Unless you cooperate, he'll try again. You know too much for him to let you live."

"No!" Alice protested with a sudden cry. "I don't believe it! Cyrus would never harm me!"

"Think not?" Starbuck's gaze narrowed. "Then who sent them? Suppose you tell me that."

"I have no idea," Alice murmured, sobbing into her hanky. "I only know it wasn't Cyrus."

"You're lying!" Starbuck said abrasively. "You sleep around, and your affairs end up with dead men all over the place. So cut the crocodile tears and dry your eyes! I don't buy your act anymore."

"Hold on, now!" Carver interjected. "I won't allow you to talk to my daughter that way!"

"Button your lip," Starbuck warned him. "Your daughter's virtue doesn't interest me. I'm only interested in *who* she's slept with! So stay the hell out of it and let her speak for herself."

Starbuck disliked the cruel sound of his voice. Yet the girl's confession was essential to the case, and he was determined to make her talk. He looked at her now with a cold stare.

A strained stillness fell over the dressing room. Alice Carver's face drained of color and she blinked, as though somewhere within herself a festering conflict had at last been resolved. Then she dabbed at her tears and took hold of herself. She sat straighter, lifted her chin defiantly, and the transformation was startling. She gave Starbuck a look that could have drawn blood.

"Very well," she said stiffly, her lips white. "Ask your questions."

"Tell me about Skinner," Starbuck prompted. "How did you get involved with him?"

"Through George Hoyt." Her eyes shuttled away. "George and I began keeping company soon after our act opened in Virginia City. He was considerate and lots of fun, and we had good times together. Then one night he introduced me to Cyrus."

"So you dropped Hoyt?" Starbuck goaded her. "Even though you knew he was stuck on you?"

"Yes, I did!" she snapped. "I never made any promises! Besides, I have a perfect right to choose who I—"

"We know what you do," Starbuck said caustically. "I take it Skinner was smitten by your charms and vice versa?"

"What of it?" Her cheeks burned with a blush. "Cyrus Skinner is a very attractive man . . . very kind."

"Save it for your diary!" Starbuck's face toughened and he squinted at her. "How long before you found out Skinner was involved in stage holdups and dirty politics?"

"I was never certain." Her look belied her words. "Not until that last night."

"The night Skinner ordered Hoyt to fake your murder?"

"Yes." Her voice was unnaturally grave, subdued. "Omar Stimson came to Cyrus's home—"

"Where were you?"

A pulse throbbed in her neck. "In the bedroom."

"What happened next?"

"Stimson was raving." Her lips trembled slightly. "He started shouting about vice collections and robberies, and how he was being cheated on the split. Before Cyrus could stop him, he mentioned something about the boss—"

"Wait a minute!" Starbuck was suddenly very quiet, eyes boring into her. "What boss? Who was he talking about?"

"I don't know." She squirmed uncomfortably in her chair. "He was just threatening to go see the 'boss.' Apparently it's someone Cyrus reports to on their . . . business affairs."

"All right, go on with what you were saying."

"Cyrus slapped him and told him someone else was in the house. They argued a little while, and then Stimson stormed out in a rage. Afterward, Cyrus was very upset, concerned for me. He said we couldn't trust Stimson to keep quiet."

"He thought Stimson might go to the 'boss' and tell him you'd overheard the conversation?"

"Something like that." She smiled wanly, remembering. "Of course, Stimson never actually saw me. But Cyrus was afraid to take the chance. He said if Stimson talked, then I would never leave Virginia City alive."

Starbuck let out his breath in a low whistle. "Now it all ties together. Skinner rigged it with Hoyt to fake your death. Then Hoyt spread the story that it was the work of outlaws trying to murder him. So that got you off the hook and it left Omar Stimson with nothing to tell the 'boss.' Isn't that about the gist of it?"

Alice Carver's hand darted to her hair like a dying bird. "Cyrus loved me very much. He jeopardized himself for my sake . . . and what we'd shared."

"No question about it," Doc Carver added hastily. "Skinner arranged the whole thing and got us out of town that same night. His only condition was that we were never to tell anyone—and stay away from Virginia City."

Starbuck heaved himself to his feet. "Doc, your secret's safe with me. You and Alice just keep quiet, and don't worry about a thing. I'll see to it you're never bothered again."

"What about Skinner?" Carver asked gloomily. "Will you have to . . ."

"I'll do my damnedest to take him alive. That's the best I can promise."

Starbuck departed on that note. Outside the dressing room, he walked toward the stage entrance. His mind turned to train schedules and the journey ahead. He figured tonight's killings had bought him a week's grace, no more. Once the news hit Virginia City, all bets were off. He would have lost the element of surprise, and the edge.

The night watchman nodded as Starbuck opened the door and stepped into the chill night air. He ran full tilt into Bill Cody. The scout stumbled and almost lost his balance. He was glassy-eyed and clearly feeling no pain. He gave Starbuck a tipsy grin.

"You're all set, Luke! I let those reporters have an earful!"

"Wish I could've been there to hear it, Bill."

"Ol' Deadeye Starbuck!" Cody laughed uproariously. "You're gonna have yourself one helluva write-up in tomorrow's papers. Course, it won't do my show any harm, either. I took a modest share of the credit—knowing you wouldn't mind."

"Don't mind a bit," Starbuck said earnestly. "You showed plenty of guts tonight, Bill. I couldn't have done it without you."

Cody's chest swelled and he stood a little straighter. "Guess I didn't do so bad at that. I've been shooting blanks so long I almost forgot what real gunpowder smells like."

"An old war-horse like you never forgets."

"Well, it's damn white of you to say so, Luke! Why don't I buy you a drink and we'll swap a few windies?"

"Another time, maybe. I've got a train to catch."

"Where the devil you off to now?"

"Headed west," Starbuck said with an odd smile. "Look me up whenever you're in Denver."

Cody wrung his hand and smote him across the shoulder. Then Starbuck turned and hurried toward the street. As he walked away it occurred to him that he had played into luck with Buffalo Bill's Combination. Tonight's backstage drama had positively identified the man he'd been hired to kill. Only one man knew about Alice Carver's empty coffin. Therefore, only one man could have sent the killers to Chicago. A man who was called boss by Virginia City's underworld leaders.

His name was Henry Palmer.

Chapter Thirteen

The east end of Wallace Street was blocked by a shoulder-to-shoulder horde of miners. The crowd choked the intersection, and the roofs of several business establishments were packed with men. Their attention was riveted on the sheriff's office.

Farther upstreet, the noon stage slowly ground to a halt. Starbuck stepped from the coach, and his gaze was immediately drawn to the commotion. He'd departed Chicago six days ago, and he looked somewhat the worse for wear. His eyes were bloodshot from too little sleep and his features were etched with fatigue. He stared at the massed throng with a fuzzy expression, thoroughly bewildered. After collecting his warbag, he stopped a miner hurrying past. The man responded to his inquiry with a shout and a huge grin.

"Hanging! Frank Yeager's gonna swing!"

The reply jolted Starbuck out of his funk. A surge of adrenalin pumped through him and he was suddenly galvanized with energy. He ducked into the hotel and left his warbag with the desk clerk. Then he crossed to the south side of the street and rushed along the boardwalk. Halfway down the block the crowd grew denser, with miners packed into a solid wedge.

He pushed and shoved, bulling through their ranks, and finally fought his way to the intersection. The sheriff's office and the jail were on the opposite corner. To the rear of the building, on an open plot of ground, stood a timbered scaffold. Several armed deputies held the crowd at a distance.

A hush fell over the miners as Starbuck edged around the corner. He stopped, staring intently across the street. Frank Yeager, arms strapped to his sides, was positioned over the gallows trapdoor. Apparently the death warrant had been read and the condemned man had already spoken his last words. As Starbuck watched, the sheriff loosened a hangman's noose dangling from the crossbeam. Palmer then slipped the noose over Yeager's head and cinched the knot tight behind the left ear. Yeager's eyes glistened and his labored breathing was audible in the eerie quiet. He looked like a bayed animal, paralyzed and desperate.

Palmer walked to the rear of the gallows and halted beside a long wooden lever. His expression was phlegmatic, no trace of emotion. He seemed to hesitate for an interminable length of time, though only a few seconds elapsed. Then he took hold of the wooden lever and yanked it hard. The trapdoor popped open and Frank Yeager shot through the hole. A split second later he hit the end of the rope with a suddenness that jarred the scaffold. His neck snapped and his head crooked over his shoulder at a grotesque angle. His body hung on a plumb line, swaying gently to the creak of the rope. A dark stain spread over the crotch of his trousers.

Somewhere in the crowd a man loosed a yipping

cheer. The assemblage took up the cry, and within moments the voices of a thousand or more miners were raised in a thunderous bloodroar. On the scaffold, Palmer seemed wholly oblivious to the bedlam on the street. He knelt at the edge of the trapdoor and felt for a pulsebeat on Yeager's neck. Then he stood, motioning to a couple of the deputies, who hurried beneath the scaffold and lifted the dead man into the air. Palmer removed the noose, and the body was lowered to the ground. The crowd began chanting his name as he descended the gallows steps. The sheriff waved and disappeared through the back door of the jail.

A chill settled over Starbuck. Something was all wrong here, and he had no ready explanation. Frank Yeager should not have gone quietly to his death. He should have accused, instead, the man who'd hanged him. The boss of Virginia City, Henry Palmer. Yet it was clear that Yeager had suspected nothing. Nor was there any evidence of hostility among the miners and townspeople. The crowd had actually cheered the sheriff.

Starbuck turned and walked away. A prickly uneasiness pervaded his thoughts, and he felt curiously disoriented. The case had taken a queer and totally unexpected twist while he was in Chicago. He needed information, details and hard facts. Only then could he sort things out and decide on his next move. He drifted along as the crowd quickly dispersed to saloons and gaming dens upstreet. A hanging was always good for business.

By the time he entered the hotel, Starbuck had re-

gained his composure. His features were a mask of
bonhomie and jolly good humor. He approached the
front desk, where he'd left his warbag, with a confident stride. He nodded pleasantly to the desk clerk.

"You missed a helluva show!"

"Just my luck!" the desk clerk grouched. "Biggest
thing that's happened around here since Heck was a
pup!"

Starbuck thought there was little chance he would
be recognized. On previous stopovers at the hotel,
he'd been operating under the guise of Lee Hall; today
he was himself. The desk clerk seemed the talkative
sort, and the lobby was empty. He figured it was as
good a place as any to start asking questions. He
leaned on the counter, his expression quizzical.

"Who was the jaybird they hung?"

"Frank Yeager!" the desk clerk said importantly.
"Only the top dog of a gang of stage robbers and
murderers!"

"No joke?" Starbuck marveled. "How'd he get
himself caught?"

"Sheriff Palmer captured him and brought him to
trial. He confessed, and the jury sentenced him to
hang."

"Confessed?" Starbuck repeated, genuinely aston-
ished. "Why would he do a thing like that?"

The desk clerk chortled. "There's a rumor the sheriff put a gun to his head. Anyway, Yeager wrote it
out and signed it, and he named names. Set the whole
town back on its ear!"

"You talking about gang members?"

"Well, that was only part of it. Turns out a couple

of big muckamucks here in town were involved. One was Omar Stimson, owned the Gem Theater. The other was Cyrus Skinner—and that really blew the lid!"

Starbuck took a tight grip on himself. "What's so important about Skinner?"

"Everybody thought he was the pillar of the community! But Yeager accused him of being the mastermind behind the robberies *and* the political kingfish of Virginia City. Appears he was right, too! Skinner lit out and he hasn't been heard from since."

"What happened to the other one . . . Stimson?"

"Dead and buried! Sheriff Palmer cornered him in his office, over at the Gem. The damn fool resisted arrest—pulled a gun—and the sheriff shot him down on the spot. Guess he figured he'd hang anyway, so what the hell!"

"How about the gang?"

"Now there's a story!"

The desk clerk gleefully recounted events of the past twenty-four hours. A news story had appeared yesterday regarding a private detective and a shootout in Chicago. The story implied that the stageline had little faith in the sheriff; thus an undercover agent had been assigned to the case. Adding to the controversy was the fact that the sheriff had captured Yeager but none of the gang. The vigilantes had mobilized, with their leader, Wilbur X. Lott, issuing a call for citizen justice. Late yesterday three gang members had been run to earth and summarily hanged. Earlier today two more robbers had been taken prisoner, and they were scheduled to hang before sundown. It was both an object lesson to outlaws and a direct challenge to the sheriff. The vigilantes planned to hold a public necktie party on the edge of town. Their act, in effect, would place them above the law.

"The town's divided," the desk clerk concluded. "Some support the sheriff and some support the vigilantes. God knows where it'll end!"

Starbuck thought it an appropriate comment. He signed the register and collected his warbag. Then he climbed the stairs and moved along the hallway to his room. His carefree manner vanished the moment the door closed. He was now thoroughly confounded.

Standing at the window, he stared out across the mining camp. He mentally catalogued all he'd learned in Chicago. The Carver girl's story, added to the backstage shootout, led inexorably to one conclusion. Sheriff Henry Palmer was the shadowy "boss" of Virginia City.

Yet that certitude had now gone by the boards. Palmer's actions over the past week or so were those of a dedicated lawman. He had wrung a confession out of Yeager and brought the gang leader to trial in open court. At the same time, he had exposed the town's vice lord and killed him in a gunfight. Finally, he'd put Cyrus Skinner to flight and thereby scuttled the entire conspiracy. All of which would have proved suicidal—if Palmer actually was the "boss."

Any of the men involved, particularly Stimson and Skinner, could have turned the tables. By identifying Palmer, they could have saved themselves and gained revenge in one stroke. But none of them had pointed an accusing finger and no allegations had been directed at the sheriff. Events, it appeared, were at variance with everything unearthed in Chicago. Nothing jibed, and for all practical purposes there was no case. The theory about Henry Palmer had been scotched.

Starbuck found himself in a quandary. There was no doubt whatever that a conspiracy existed. Alice Carver's story, in that respect at least, had been borne out by what he'd uncovered on his own. Yet the principal suspect—until an hour ago the only suspect—was seemingly absolved of guilt. Which raised the specter of still another imponderable.

Who was the phantom "boss" of Virginia City?

Late that afternoon the sun slowly retreated toward the mountains. The creek was molten with sunlight and the road through Alder Gulch was jammed with miners. Their destination was a clearing on the outskirts of town.

Starbuck was lost in the crowd. He estimated there were easily twice as many men as had attended Frank Yeager's hanging. More were arriving by the minute, with a greater number from claims upstream along the gulch. The turnout indicated the vigilantes had mustered strong support.

From his vantage point, Starbuck had what amounted to a ringside seat. He stood on a small knoll which directly overlooked the clearing. A large alder tree, with massive branches sweeping outward, dominated the scene. He thought it ironic that the alder had already been dubbed the Judas Tree. The Judas he sought, who was still unidentified, no doubt appreciated the joke even more. Understandably, the vigilantes had selected the name solely for its biblical symbolism. All who robbed and murdered their fellow men were by definition the worst of traitors. Or so the vigilantes claimed.

Strangely, Starbuck was not an advocate of vigilante justice. He hunted down outlaws and killed them, which was a form of summary execution. Yet he operated within the framework of the law, and he considered it contemptible to kill in cold blood. By his code, a mob was never to be trusted. There was no reason in their ugliness, no temperance in their rage.

Some years ago, on his first job as a range detective, he'd witnessed the madness of mob action. Hired by a group of ranchers, he had trailed a gang of horse thieves to No Man's Land. Following a gun battle, the ranchers had hanged the surviving gang members in a frenzy of bloodlust. With no power to intervene, he had gone along, even participated in the lynching. But he'd thought less of himself in the aftermath, and he hadn't slept well for some months. Since then, he had avoided vigilantes like a virulent disease.

Today he was reminded of that long-ago incident. In the clearing below, a group of some twenty vigilantes were gathered around the alder tree. Wilbur X. Lott, their leader, was busily orchestrating the proceedings. A cadaverous man, with a hooked nose and a downturned mouth, he was attired in a hammertail coat and a high-crowned black hat. His voice was loud and astringent, like that of a schoolteacher instructing unruly children. Which was not too far from the truth. He was teaching the rudiments of slow and painful death.

The men waiting to be hanged were apparently resigned to the ordeal. Their hands were tied behind their backs and their expressions were vacant, almost bovine. One of the robbers was Yeager's lieutenant, Charley Reeves. The other man was a hapless gang member whose name meant nothing to anyone. With seeming indifference, they allowed themselves to be positioned beneath a stout tree limb. Then ropes were tossed over the limb and crude nooses were fitted around their necks. Several vigilantes stepped forward and took hold of the slack ropes. Oddly, they looked like teams about to engage in a tug-of-war.

On Lott's command, the vigilantes hauled back on the ropes. The robbers, dancing frantically on empty space, were hoisted off the ground. Their eyes bulged and seemed to burst from the sockets with engorged blood vessels. Their gyrations spun them kicking and thrashing, while their features purpled, then turned darker. Their mouths popped open and their swollen tongues gradually changed from blackish amber to deep onyx in color. They vainly fought the ropes until the last gasp of air was gone, and even then their frenzied struggles lessened only by degrees. Several minutes passed while they slowly strangled to death.

Starbuck eased through the crowd and made his way back to the road. As he walked toward town it occurred to him that Wilbur X. Lott was either a rank amateur or an inhuman sadist. He tended to think it was the latter. Lott had staged a gruesome spectacle with only one thought in mind. After today, the vigilante leader would be known as a fearsome avenger, the champion of honest men. It was a reputation that would serve him well when he threw his hat into the political arena. The hanging of the stagecoach robbers was strictly incidental. A sideshow to beguile the mob and win support.

On the edge of town, Starbuck spotted Henry Palmer. The sheriff was standing outside a whorehouse on the fringe of the red-light district. From there, he had observed the mass gathering of miners and the hangings. That he hadn't attended—or attempted to interfere—was a gauge of the mood in Virginia City. His expression was somber as he watched Starbuck approach.

"Hello, Luke." He nodded stiffly. "Heard you'd checked into the hotel."

"I got back in time to see Frank Yeager take the drop."

"Why didn't you come by the office?"

Starbuck ignored the question. "That was a nifty piece of work with Yeager. From what I hear, you got him to squeal like a stuck hog."

"Nothing to brag about," Palmer said, no timbre in his voice. "I should've followed your advice—gone after Stimson's bouncer."

"What stopped you?"

"Figured I'd make Yeager talk and build a stronger case. It worked fine till things went haywire."

Starbuck eyed him keenly. "Stimson's bouncer wasn't around, anyway. He trailed me to Chicago."

"I read about it." Palmer shook his head ruefully.

"Guess we outfoxed ourselves. Stimson must've had a tail on you the whole time."

"Appears that way."

"How'd you do with Alice Carver?"

"Blind alley." Starbuck opened hs hands, shrugged. "She wasn't with her father, and all my other leads fizzled out. I suppose she'll turn up someday."

"Yeah, probably so." Palmer hawked and spat, eyes rimmed with disgust. "Seems like tough breaks always come in bunches."

Starbuck looked down and studied the ground a moment. "What're you doing about Skinner?"

"I've put out feelers." Palmer's face twisted in a grimace. "If he's still in Montana, I'll hear about it."

"You really think he'd stick around?"

"No," Palmer said with a sour look. "I'd say he's far away and still running."

"Wouldn't surprise me." Starbuck arched one eyebrow. "How'd Stimson come to pull a gun on you?"

"Your guess on that's as good as mine. I thought he'd go along peaceable, and instead he made a fight of it. I was lucky to get him before he got me."

"Too bad," Starbuck remarked. "He would've made a better witness than Yeager."

"Too bad and too late," Palmer added without humor. "By the time I got to Skinner's office, the news was already out. He skipped town one step ahead of me."

"Word travels fast," Starbuck said evenly. "What about the Judas . . . anything turn up?"

"No hard proof." Palmer seemed to look through him. "But I'd bet my bottom dollar it was Skinner.

His assay business gave him all sorts of inside information. Course, the way things sit, we'll probably never know."

"I reckon not." Starbuck nodded absently. "How do you figure to stop the vigilantes?"

"I don't." Palmer regarded him with great calmness. "I couldn't deputize enough men to stop them. Besides, it'll eventually run its course anyhow. Wilbur Lott won't be able to hold them together."

"He seems to be doing a pretty fair job so far."

"A couple of days don't mean a thing. A week from now it'll all be ancient history."

"Hope you're right." Starbuck gave him a sideways look. "If you're not, it's liable to get ugly. Vigilantes generally wind up lynching innocent people before they're through."

"I almost wish they would!" Palmer said fiercely. "Then I'd have an excuse to stretch Wilbur Lott's skinny neck!"

"Write me and let me how how it turns out."

Palmer looked surprised. "That sounds like you're calling it quits?"

"No reason to stay." Starbuck's smile was cryptic. "Skinner's the only one left alive, and he's long gone. I reckon I'll just close the file on this one. I've got other fish to fry."

"Another case?"

"Sheriff, there's always another case!"

Starbuck pumped hs hand vigorously and walked off toward town. He wondered if Palmer realized he'd lied not once but several times during the conversation. Then, with a sardonic chuckle, he put it from mind. He had a fish to fry that wouldn't wait.

A sucker fish otherwise known as Cyrus Skinner.

Chapter Fourteen

The night was cold and dark. Starbuck stood in the alley behind the Alder Gulch Assay Company. With the butt of his Colt, he broke an upper pane of glass in the rear window. He listened intently for a moment before holstering the pistol. Then he slipped his hand through the broken pane and unlocked the window catch.

A burlap bag lay at his feet. Inside were various tools he'd purchased earlier at a hardware store. After raising the window, he pushed the bag through and lowered it to the floor. He climbed over the sill, then closed the window and drew the blind. The door to the room was shut, and a quick look around convinced him he was in Cyrus Skinner's private office. He pulled a candle from his pocket and lit it with a match. Directly opposite him was a squat floor safe, positioned against the wall. Grunting with satisfaction, he dripped hot wax on the edge of a nearby desk and sealed the candle in place. Then he opened the bag of tools and went to work.

The break-in had been prompted by several factors. A remark by Henry Palmer during their conversation that afternoon had provided the key. The sheriff, immediately after killing Stimson, had gone from the theater to Skinner's office. But word of the shooting had preceded him, and he found Skinner had already skipped town. Which meant Skinner had been caught unprepared, with no time to organize his escape. He'd taken flight on the spur of the moment.

Starbuck understood the criminal mentality. Over the years, he'd developed the knack of stepping into the other man's boots and viewing a situation from the crook's perspective. Everything he had learned to date indicated Cyrus Skinner was a careful man, a methodical planner. So it was reasonable to assume Skinner would have prepared—in advance—for any eventuality. In particular, he would have taken steps to secure his financial position. He would not have fled into poverty.

Yet an assay business was hardly a conduit for large amounts of gold. It followed, then, that Skinner would have developed a method for disposing of the stolen bullion. Starbuck was less interested in the method than in where the gold had gone. He felt confident that when he found the gold he would find Skinner. Since there had been no time to destroy records, Skinner had very probably left behind a paper trail. A file, or perhaps a ledger, that would lead ultimately to a bank. From there, it would be only a matter of legwork to locate Skinner himself. A thief and his money were seldom far apart.

Starbuck's plan was simple. Tonight's job would appear the work of a common yeggman. No one would suspect he'd looted the office, and there would be nothing to indicate the actual purpose of the rob-

bery. He attacked the safe with a drill punch and a
four-foot crowbar. Within ten minutes, he had peeled
the safe door and was pawing through the contents.
He found more than he'd expected.

The stolen gold was on deposit at a bank in Salt
Lake City. There was a ledger indicating the dates of
deposit and a current balance in excess of one hundred
thousand dollars. Stuck inside the ledger was a dossier
on one Robert Dempsey. Documented therein was evidence that Dempsey had murdered his former partner
in a mining venture; the spot where the body had been
buried was clearly marked on an enclosed map. On
the map as well were directions to a spot identified
simply as Dempsey's Cabin. Some twenty miles south
of Virginia City, the cabin was located on Stinkingwater Creek.

Starbuck puzzled on it for several minutes. Then,
suddenly, he grasped the significance of the dossier
and map. The man named Robert Dempsey was Skinner's conduit for the stolen gold. The bullion was
somehow transferred to Dempsey, and he in turn arranged to deposit it with the bank in Salt Lake City.
But Skinner was apparently a cautious man and operated on the principle that there was no honor among
thieves. He'd gathered evidence of the old murder and
used it as an instrument of blackmail against Dempsey. He thereby ensured that the gold would arrive
safely in Salt Lake City. At the same time, he had
guaranteed Dempsey's silence.

Cyrus Skinner's vanishing act was no longer a
mystery. Whether or not he'd gone on to Salt Lake

City was a moot point. His first stop was pinpointed precisely on the map.

A cabin on Stinkingwater Creek.

The sun was at its zenith. A narrow ribbon of water snaked through a boulder-strewn canyon. On one side of the creek, the shoreline was sheltered by trees. On the other, a crude log cabin was silhouetted against distant mountains. Smoke drifted lazily from the chimney.

Starbuck lay concealed in the trees. By the angle of the sun, he judged he'd been watching the cabin for nearly an hour. No one had appeared during that time, even though the cabin was clearly occupied. He took heart from the fact that there were two horses standing hipshot in a split-log corral. One man rarely had need of an extra mount.

The wait was slowly beginning to wear on his nerves. He'd ridden through the night, following the road south from Virginia City. Early that morning he had hit Stinkingwater Creek and left his horse tied in a grove of trees. On foot, he had then made his way upstream, pausing frequently to check the map. After spotting the cabin, he'd bellied down and wormed the last hundred yards. He was now bone-tired and on edge, and toying with the idea of rushing the cabin. He decided to give it another five minutes.

The cabin door abruptly opened and a man stepped outside. Starbuck watched as he walked toward the creek with a bucket. He was large and burly, and in no way fitted the description of Cyrus Skinner. Which pretty well pegged him as Skinner's secret accomplice, Robert Dempsey. A pistol was strapped on his hip, and the holster shifted higher as he stooped down at the creek. He dipped the bucket into the water.

"Don't move!"

Starbuck's command was rapped out in a hard voice. Dempsey froze for an instant; then he dropped the bucket and dodged sideways. He moved uncommonly fast for a big man, and the pistol appeared in his hand before he'd taken a full step. He suddenly stopped in his tracks, whirling and crouching, and fired blindly at the treeline. Starbuck shot him twice, centering both shots within a handspan of his shirt pocket. The slugs jarred him backward and his bootheel caught on a rock. Then the gun fell from his hand and he spraddled out on the creek bank. He lay perfectly still.

On his belly, Starbuck squirmed a few yards upstream and took cover behind another tree. He watched the cabin for several moments and thought he saw a shadow of movement behind the window. He cupped one hand to his mouth and yelled.

"Skinner!" He waited a beat. "I know you're in there. Let's talk!"

A long moment slipped past. Then, his voice muffled from within the cabin, Skinner called out. "Who are you?"

"Luke Starbuck! I'm a private detective—the stage-line hired me!"

"How do I know you won't kill me?"

"Doc Carver asked me to take you alive! I promised I'd try!"

"Carver?" Skinner sounded doubtful. "What's it to him?"

"His daughter's still sweet on you! Besides, he figures they owe you one for getting them out of town!"

"Why should I believe you?"

"You've got no choice!" Starbuck replied. "You can come out and live. Or I'll burn you out and kill you. Take your pick!"

Skinner hesitated only briefly. "All right, you win! I'm throwing my gun out. Don't shoot!"

The cabin door opened and Skinner tossed his revolver on the ground. Then he took a tentative step outside and halted, hands raised overhead. He stared apprehensively at the treeline.

Starbuck scrambled to his feet. He kept Skinner covered and cautiously forded the creek. As he moved closer he saw why Alice Carver had lost her head. Skinner was an unusually handsome man. His features had a chiseled look, with a cleft in his chin and piercing dark eyes. His hair was raven black and wavy, and he was built along lithe, muscular lines. He was a ladies' man who looked the part.

"How did you find me?" Skinner asked nervously. "I never told anyone about Dempsey."

"Tricks of the trade," Starbuck said with a tired smile. "You might say I followed a paper trail."

Skinner appeared bemused. "Alice couldn't have told you—she didn't know!"

"She told me lots of other things."

"Such as?"

"The whole setup," Starbuck said matter-of-factly. "How do you think I got onto your game?"

"What game?"

"The stage holdups," Starbuck observed. "Your political connections. You and Stimson and Yeager. . . . everything."

"I don't believe you!" Skinner said in an aggrieved tone. "It wasn't Alice! You got to me through Yeager."

Starbuck shrugged, watching his eyes. "When did you learn I was on the case?"

"The night—" Skinner stopped, shook his head. "Good try! I never heard your name before today."

"Believe it or not," Starbuck countered, "I'm trying to pull your fat out of the fire. Alice also told me about your boss."

Skinner gave him a blank stare. "What boss?"

"You sure loused it up," Starbuck went on with a mirthless grin. "He must've been some ticked off when he found out you'd faked the Carver girl's death."

"I don't know what you're talking about."

"You've got one chance." Starbuck's voice dropped. "Tell me his name—turn state's evidence— and let me go after him. Otherwise, you'll wind up in the bone-yard."

"Oh?" Skinner blustered. "What makes you think so?"

"You're the last witness!" Starbuck said urgently. "The only one who knows the full story. He means to kill you and he'll do it—unless I stop him."

Skinner glanced away and stared for a long while at nothing. He was quiet so long Starbuck began to think he wouldn't answer. But finally he sighed and spread his hands wide. His face was stricken with a look of dread and uncertainty.

"All right," he conceded glumly. "I'll make a deal with you. Deliver me to the territorial capital and put me in the custody of the attorney general. Then I'll tell you anything you want to know."

Starbuck examined the notion. "Helena's a long way off. Why not tell me now?"

"I want insurance." Skinner grinned weakly. "You get me there alive and I'll talk! Not before."

A moment elapsed while they stared at one another. Then Starbuck nodded. "You've got yourself a deal. We'll spend the night in Virginia City and catch the morning stage. That ought to put us into Helena day after tomorrow."

"No!" Skinner's eyes froze to pinpoints of darkness. "I won't go back to Virginia City!"

"Don't worry," Starbuck said with a clenched smile. "I won't let him get you."

"I refuse!" Skinner's voice was choked with terror. "I'm as good as dead the minute I set foot in town!"

"Quit squawking!" Starbuck silenced him with a frown. "You're my prisoner, and nobody will harm you while you're in my custody."

"He'll try," Skinner whispered desperately. "You know he'll try!"

"I know he's dead if he does."

Starbuck considered it a no-lose proposition. By returning to Virginia City, he might end the case quickly and permanently. Helena would delay things a few days, but time was now on his side. Either way, he'd gained the edge at last.

He went along to the corral while Skinner saddled a horse.

Dusk was settling over Virginia City. Starbuck and Skinner rode into town as the last rays of light were leached from the sky. Their arrival was timed perfectly with the supper hour and onrushing darkness. The streets were virtually empty.

Starbuck thought it wiser to bypass the livery stable. The sooner he got Skinner undercover, the better. Then, if an assassination attempt was made, it would be made on ground of his own choosing. He led Skinner to the hotel and they dismounted out front. As they moved to the hitch rack, he heard a coarse shout from across the street. He looked around, and his blood went cold.

Wilbur X. Lott and a group of vigilantes had just emerged from a café. With hardly a break in stride, they stepped off the boardwalk and hurried toward the hotel. Their eyes were fastened on Skinner, and the look on their faces was the look of death. A cone of silence enveloped them as they approached in a tight phalanx.

Too late, Starbuck realized his mistake. The focus of his concentration had been on one man, a lone killer. He'd forgotten that a pack of killers now roamed the streets of Virginia City. A lynch-crazed pack, sworn to hang Cyrus Skinner. He felt slow and stupid, and he silently cursed himself. In his rush to get one man, he'd overlooked the greater danger. The mob.

Lott halted directly in front of him. The vigilantes spread out and slowly surrounded the hitch rack. Skinner's features turned ashen and he unwittingly moved closer to Starbuck. Lott uttered a dry laugh that sounded like a death rattle.

"Well, now, Mr. Starbuck! You are a detective, aren't you?"

"Skinner's my prisoner." Starbuck's eyes went steely. "I won't turn him over, Lott. So call off your dogs."

"Why should we fight?" Lott's face was a mask of righteous propriety. "A man in your profession understands the need for summary justice. Our goals are the same, Mr. Starbuck."

"Shove it!" Starbuck's voice was alive with contempt. "I work my own game, and it's not done yet. I've still got need of Skinner."

"That's unfortunate," Lott replied with cold hauteur. "You see, we want to ask him a few questions ourselves. I suggest you stand aside."

Starbuck's mouth clamped in a bloodless line. "Why don't you try moving me aside?"

"Come now!" Lott scoffed. "You're in a hopeless position, Mr. Starbuck. Unless, of course, you're willing to die just to make a point."

The snout of a pistol jabbed into Starbuck's spine. He stared at Lott, his look dark and vengeful. Then, with an effort of will, he forced himself to nod, signifying he'd lost. Lott laughed and motioned to his men with a brusque gesture.

"Bring them both along," he ordered. "I think Mr. Starbuck might learn something."

Lott walked off upstreet. The vigilantes crowded around Starbuck and Skinner, and they fell in behind. Several minutes later they entered the clearing on the outskirts of town. The Judas Tree stood bathed in a spectral glow of starlight. The ropes from yesterday's hangings still dangled over the limb, and there was a ghoulish aspect to the scene. A man was assigned to watch Starbuck, and others hustled Skinner beneath the tree. After a noose was slipped around his neck, several vigilantes took hold of the rope. Then Lott stepped forward and faced him.

"Cyrus, you're going to die." He spoke the words with a kind of smothered wrath. "How you die depends on whether or not you cooperate."

Skinner stood numb with shock. "I—I've done nothing."

Lott glanced past him and gestured. The rope snapped taut and Skinner was snatched off the ground. He clawed wildly at the noose, which cut deeper into his throat as the weight of his body pulled the loop ever tighter. His eyes were maddened and bulging, vivid with pain. He kicked and jerked, dancing on thin air, and his face turned a dark shade of purple. Then, at a signal from Lott, the vigilantes abruptly released the rope. Skinner dropped on the ground and fell to his knees. He tore the noose free and sucked wind into his starved lungs. He gagged, clutching at his throat, and coughed raggedly. His breathing was a labored wheeze in the still night.

"Cyrus, that's only a sample," Lott warned with cold menace. "You'll die by inches unless you give me a full confession."

"No more!" Skinner pleaded hoarsely. "I'll talk—I swear it!"

"A wise decision," Lott intoned. "I have only one question, so pay very close attention. Tell me about Henry Palmer."

"He's the boss! He fed me the information about the express shipments, and I passed it along to Stimson and Yeager. He controlled everything . . . all of us!"

"Where did he get the information?"

"The express company," Skinner babbled. "He's the sheriff . . . they never suspected anything . . . he was hanging robbers . . . they let him see the shipment schedules . . . so he could catch more robbers."

"These robbers he hung?" Lott demanded. "Were they part of the gang?"

"Only a con game . . . make everybody think there wasn't a gang!"

"Why didn't Yeager spill all that during his trial?"

"Yeager didn't know! No one but Stimson and me knew about Palmer. That's why he killed Stimson . . . resisting arrest . . . would've killed me, too. But I fooled him, got away!"

"How about politics?" Lott persisted. "Who controlled the county machine?"

"Palmer!" Skinner rasped. "It was always Palmer! I was only his front man. He organized it . . . pulled the strings . . . through me!"

"Thank you, Cyrus." Lott grinned an evil grin. "You've confirmed everything I suspected right along. Now, for the record, I have one final question. Do you swear before almighty God that you've told the whole truth?"

"Yes!" Skinner's eyes filled with panic. "With Christ as my witness—I do!"

"Good," Lott said viciously. "Hang him!"

Skinner threw up a hand, palm outward. His mouth opened in protest and then clicked shut in a strangled gasp. The vigilantes heaved on the rope and jerked him off his knees. Another tug lifted him into the air, his arms and legs flapping in a spastic struggle. A rictus of agony crossed his features and he wet his pants. His hands dug insanely at the noose.

The man guarding Starbuck edged closer. His eyes were bright with fascination, and Skinner's death struggles seemed to compel him forward. He took another step and another, transfixed by the sight. Then, all else forgotten, he stood staring upward, spellbound.

Starbuck turned and vanished into the darkness.

Chapter Fifteen

A single lamp lighted the sheriff's office. Starbuck angled across the street and gingerly stepped onto the boardwalk. He pulled the Colt, thumbing the hammer to full cock. Then he catfooted toward the door.

Outside, he paused and flattened himself against the wall. One ear cocked to the door, he listened for several seconds. There was no sound from within, and the silence sparked a vague feeling of unease. He took a firm grip on the doorknob and braced himself. The door creaked as he threw it open and extended the Colt to arm's length. The office was empty.

Still wary, he moved through the doorway and stopped just inside. He slammed the door shut and stood for a moment, scanning the room. The desk was littered with paperwork, and a potbellied stove crackled with warmth. Everything appeared normal, and yet a curious sense of desolation pervaded the office. He collected the lamp from the desk and walked swiftly to the door of the lockup. All the cells were empty; the barred doors along the corridor yawned open. He returned to the office and slowly holstered the Colt. His expression was troubled.

Some inner voice told Starbuck the worst had hap-

pened. There were no deputies around and the jail-
house was deserted. All the signs indicated the office
had been vacated hurriedly, sometime within the last
hour. He thought it entirely probable that the sheriff
had gotten word of Skinner's capture. Further, with
Skinner in the hands of the vigilantes, it would be
logical to assume that the last link in the conspiracy
had been revealed. Cyrus Skinner, in an attempt to
save himself, would spill his guts about the "boss" of
Virginia City. Which meant Henry Palmer would
have been under no illusions about his own fate. He
was the next candidate for the Judas Tree.

Starbuck was gripped by a sense of time running
ahead of him. His eyes felt scratchy and burnt out,
and he wearily massaged them as he considered his
options. The smart move, on Palmer's part, would
have been to depart town hastily. Only by vanishing
into the night would he outdistance the hangman's
rope and certain death. In that event, Starbuck had no
choice but to pick up the trail and give chase. Yet
there loomed before him the question of where to
start. He abruptly realized that he knew virtually nothing of a personal nature about Henry Palmer. Wife
and family aside, he had no idea as to where the sheriff lived. A man's home, most assuredly, was the first
place to look. Where to ask directions, however,
posed a problem. He couldn't afford loose talk and
speculation, not with the vigilantes on the prowl. He
somehow had to cover his own tracks.

Once more outside, he turned toward the center of
town. He figured the hotel was perhaps the best place
to inquire. A gold piece, backed by a subtle threat,

would ensure the night clerk's silence. As he walked, his mind drifted unwittingly to the vigilantes. There was an inescapable note of irony, not to mention a certain rancor, in his attitude. On general principles, he detested mob justice and the element of anarchy underlying any vigilance movement. On a personal level, he burned with a quiet, steel fury toward Wilbur X. Lott. The vigilante leader had taken his prisoner at gunpoint and compounded the insult by threatening his life. He allowed no man that liberty, and sooner or later Lott would be made to pay the piper. All the more so since Starbuck considered Lott a malevolent force, no less evil than the outlaws themselves. An ambitious man was too often a sinister man, and therefore the most dangerous of all.

Still, in the end, it boiled down to a matter of priorities. Wilbur X. Lott was strictly personal business, and settling his hash would wait. In the meantime, there was a more pressing problem, one that topped Starbuck's list. He was determined that the vigilantes wouldn't beat him to Henry Palmer.

Later, looking back on the moment, Starbuck would be struck by the blend of timing and coincidence. As he approached the main intersection a group of miners emerged from the café on the corner. Their raucous laughter attracted his attention, and he stopped dead in his tracks. Through the fly-specked window he saw Palmer seated at a table inside the café. The sheriff was sopping stew gravy from his plate with a piece of bread. Even as Starbuck watched he popped the bread into his mouth and began chewing. His demeanor was that of a man without a trouble in the world.

Starbuck was immobilized by the sight. He briefly wondered if Palmer somehow hadn't heard about Skinner. Then, upon second thought, he discarded the notion. The odds dictated that Palmer had learned of Skinner's capture within minutes after it happened. Yet there he sat, calmy eating his supper. It beggared the imagination.

The supper hour was drawing to a close. All up and down the street the boardwalks were jammed with men out to see the elephant. With the exception of Palmer, only three diners still lingered in the café. Starbuck debated whether to make his play inside or risk a showdown on the crowded street. Then he saw a waitress approach the table and refill the sheriff's coffee mug. He again experienced the sensation of fleeting time. To delay might very well cut his slight lead over the vigilantes. He decided to wait no longer.

Palmer was seated at a window table, facing the door. Starbuck entered quickly and halted just inside the café. His hand was underneath his suit jacket, gripping the butt of the Colt. His gaze bored into Palmer, inviting a move. A moment passed while the two men stared at each other. Then the sheriff carefully wrapped both hands around his coffee mug. A token act, it signified he chose not to fight.

Alert to trickery, Starbuck slowly approached the table. He saw, upon moving closer, that there was a strangeness about Palmer. The sheriff's eyes were oddly vacant and his features were fixed. He had a faraway look, as though the focus of his concentration were centered on something dimly visible in the distance. He nodded to Starbuck.

"Have a chair."

"You're a regular sackful of surprises."

"How so?"

"I figured you'd fight the minute I showed."

"I don't want to kill you, Luke."

"You'll have to try"—Starbuck's tone was impersonal—"if you intend to walk out of here."

"No, I won't." Palmer paused, met his gaze with an amused expression. "There's no way you can force me to draw . . . not just yet."

Starbuck seated himself across the table. He lit a cigarette, all the while watching Palmer's hands. Then he snuffed the match and exhaled a cloud of smoke.

"What's your game?"

Palmer's smile was bleak. "You tell me your secrets and I'll tell you mine."

"Go ahead," Starbuck agreed. "Ask away."

"Have Lott and his bunch hung Skinner?"

"He was on his way up the last time I saw him."

"Did they make him talk?"

"Oh, he talked!" Starbuck took a long draw on his cigarette. "He'd still be talking if he hadn't run out of things to say."

"I suppose the questions were about me?"

"Nobody else." Starbuck spoke the words in little spurts of smoke. "Skinner identified you as the boss of Virginia City. Vice, politics, and stage holdups . . . the whole can of worms."

"I'm not surprised," Palmer said equably. "Cyrus always was short on guts."

"Why shouldn't he talk? He knew you meant to kill him the same way you killed Stimson."

"A double-crosser deserves what he gets."

Starbuck eyed him, thoughtful. "You're talking about the Carver girl, aren't you?"

"Am I?"

"Skinner tricked you," Starbuck said, not asking a question. "You thought she was dead till the night we opened the coffin."

Palmer seemed to wrestle with himself a moment. He turned the coffee mug in his hands, examining it like some curious artifact. Finally, with a great shrug of resignation, he glanced up.

"You're right." His voice was at once reasonable and tinged with anger. "Skinner played me for a sucker. The way he rigged her death—and that phony funeral—was a big mistake. He was thinking with his balls instead of his brains."

"So what?" Starbuck asked. "There was no real harm done. She never actually knew who you were."

"She knew I existed! After we dug up her coffin, I got the full story out of Stimson. Maybe she didn't know my name, but she knew too much. That's why Skinner got her out of town."

"What was the alternative?"

"He should've come to me!" Palmer replied. "What she overheard wasn't his fault. I wouldn't have held it against him."

"Probably not." Starbuck tapped an ash off his cigarette. "But you would've killed Alice Carver."

"That was Skinner's second mistake. By letting her live, he put everybody's tail in a crack."

"I'll give you credit," Starbuck said with a lightning frown. "It was a mistake you damn sure tried to correct."

"You mean that fiasco in Chicago?"

"I wouldn't exactly call it a fiasco. Another minute, and those boys would've got the girl and me *and* Doc Carver. It almost worked."

"Too little too late," Palmer said morosely. "Strictly a last-ditch effort. By then, things were unraveling so fast I was always a step behind. I lay it to George Hoyt's death."

"You didn't order him killed?"

Palmer grunted, shook his head. "Stimson took it upon himself. He got wise to you, and then his boys trailed you to Hoyt's office. He figured to wipe the slate clean—kill you both."

"So you were still in the dark at that point. You didn't know who I was till I told you myself?"

"Unfortunate, but true," Palmer affirmed. "And that's when I made my big mistake. I should've killed you out at the graveyard and buried you in that empty coffin."

"Why didn't you?"

"Tell you the truth—" Palmer paused and stared at him a long moment. "I was so goddamn mad at Skinner I wasn't thinking straight. By the time I quit seeing red, you were already on your way to Chicago."

"One thing puzzles me," Starbuck said, watching him inquisitively. "How'd you get Stimson to send his boys after me?"

"Carrot and the stick." Palmer's mouth lifted in a tight grin. "I let him think he could square himself by getting rid of you and the Carver girl. He swallowed it, bait and all."

"Meanwhile—" Starbuck gave him a short look. "You were rigging a double-cross of your own. Yeager didn't know the score, so you charged him with robbery and murder. Then you killed Stimson for resisting arrest. If you'd got Skinner, that was the game. Nobody would've been left alive to identify you."

"Almost pulled it off, too! I just never figured Skinner to run that fast. Guess he saw the handwriting on the wall."

"He wasn't in any doubt that you meant to put him under."

"How'd you find him?" Palmer said, genuinely curious. "That was a slick piece of detective work."

"It's a long story," Starbuck said flatly. "Let's stick with you for the moment. Tell me how you got the inside dope on those gold shipments."

"Wasn't all that hard," Palmer noted. "The boys over at the express office never suspected the law was behind it. I generally managed to get a peek at the shipment schedules."

"What about your deputies?" Starbuck remarked. "Were they involved?"

"No," Palmer said briskly. "I kept them busy chasing small-timers. It was good whitewash and it had everybody fooled down the line. Leastways till you showed up."

"One last question." Starbuck stubbed out his cigarette in an ashtray. "Why are you admitting all this so openly?"

There was a prolonged silence. Palmer's stare revealed nothing, and he might have been deaf for all the change in his expression. He studied Starbuck at length before answering.

"Correct me if I'm wrong," he said coolly. "You're thinking this will end one of two ways. Either Lott and his thugs hang me, or you'll do the honors. Would that be a fair statement?"

"Close enough to count."

A smile shadowed Palmer's lips. "Wilbur Lott will never hang me."

"That a fact?" Starbuck regarded him with a level gaze. "What makes you think so?"

"I'm the law!" Palmer said forcefully. "It's Cyrus Skinner's word against mine, and that's no contest. All I have to do is bluff and stick to it—and they wouldn't dare hang me!"

"So you're betting it all on one turn of the cards?"

"Why not?" Palmer said grimly. "If I run, you'd be right behind me. I'm better off to take my chances here . . . tonight."

"And if Lott doesn't hang you?"

"Then it's between us," Palmer said pointedly, "and I'll have to kill you. That's why I said you couldn't force me to draw . . . not just yet."

"In other words," Starbuck commented, "there's no need to kill me if they do end up hanging you?"

Palmer nodded gravely. "I don't kill for sport. Unless your death serves some purpose, why bother?"

"That's real charitable of you." Starbuck's gaze was very pale and direct. "For the sake of argument, let's suppose you don't hang. What makes you think

I wouldn't kill you—instead of the other way around?"

Palmer shrugged off the question. "You kill men but you don't murder them. I've never imposed such rules on myself."

"You're saying you'd backshoot me?"

"Something like that," Palmer said without irony. "Better you than me, Luke."

Not for the first time, Starbuck's admiration was stirred. The man seated opposite him was a cold-blooded cutthroat, with all the conscience of an aroused scorpion. Yet Palmer possessed icy nerves and bold cunning, the very attributes a lawman prized most. Under different circumstances they might have been allies, if not friends. Tonight, Starbuck could offer him nothing more than a quick death.

"You won't stand the chance of a snowball in hell with the vigilantes."

"I disagree," Palmer said firmly. "I've lived by my wits all my life. It won't be any chore to outfox Wilbur Lott."

"If you're wrong, it's not a pleasant way to die. He's a strangler, not a hangman."

"What's your point?"

"Draw now." Starbuck looked him square in the eye. "You'll never know what hit you."

Palmer deliberated a moment. His expression was abstracted and he seemed to be weighing the proposal. Then he slowly wagged his head.

"No soap," he said with assurance. "I'll worry about you after I've dealt with Lott."

"It's your funeral."

"What the hell!" Palmer laughed. "A high roller always plays for table stakes."

"Only one trouble."

"What's that?"

"You're playing into a cold deck."

Palmer suddenly stiffened. His eyes shifted to the window and he stared upstreet. In the erratic flicker of lamplight, he saw Lott and the vigilantes marching toward the intersection. A man in the lead rank carried a coiled rope, and one end was knotted in a hangman's noose. All along the street miners stopped and gawked as the vigilantes strode past.

"Well, Luke . . ." Palmer rose from his chair. "Time to play out the hand. Wish me luck."

"A dead man needs more than luck."

Palmer grinned and crossed the room with a determined stride. At the door he paused, squaring his shoulders; then he threw it open and stepped outside. He moved directly toward the vigilantes.

Starbuck stood and walked from the café.

Chapter Sixteen

The boardwalk outside the café was jammed with miners. Pushing through the crowd, Starbuck noted that all four corners of Wallace and Jackson were packed with ghoulish onlookers. He shouldered past the men at the front and took a position beside the lamppost. Then his attention was drawn to the street.

Henry Palmer halted in the middle of the intersection. He planted himself as though he'd taken root, legs spread wide. The shiny star pinned on his vest gleamed brightly in the lamplight. His expression was stolid and his stance was that of a monolith, somehow immovable. He threw up an arm, palm outward.

"That's far enough!" he called brassily. "You boys are through for the night!"

The vigilantes stopped several paces away. Their features registered surprise and momentary confusion. A moment of stark silence ensued while they stood immobilized by Palmer's glowering stare. On the boardwalk, the spectators appeared spellbound, watching with trancelike awe. Then Wilbur X. Lott took a step forward.

"No, by God!" Lott shouted. "We're not through! We've only just started!"

Palmer fixed him with a baleful look. "I'm ordering you to disband—now!"

"Order and be damned!" Lott said fiercely. "It's you we want, Palmer."

"On what charge?"

"Murder! Highway robbery! Contempt for the laws of man and sacrilege against a higher law—the law of God!"

"Wilbur, are you preaching a sermon?" Palmer's tone was laced with mockery. "Or maybe you're play-acting for the crowd? You always did have a flair for the dramatic."

"Save your ridicule!" Lott yelled. "It won't work! We've got the goods on you and your gang of road agents!"

"Are you asking me to believe you have proof?"

"I'm not asking!" Lott thundered. "I'm telling you! Cyrus Skinner confessed not ten minutes ago. He named you as the leader—the mastermind!"

"For the benefit of everyone here"—Palmer gestured around with a sardonic smile—"how did you extract that confession?"

"With a rope! We let him dangle till he decided to come clean!"

"Come off it, Wilbur! You put the words in his mouth and choked him until he told you what you wanted to hear. Isn't that how it happened?"

"He told us the truth! The whole truth! How you organized the gang and used him as a mouthpiece. He named you as the man responsible for the holdups and killings. The boss!"

"It won't hold water," Palmer informed him. "A

confession obtained under duress isn't admissible in court."

"We're not debating technicalities. Skinner identified you! That's all the proof we need."

"Proof?" Palmer repeated scornfully. "You hung your witness, Wilbur! All we have is your version of what you strangled out of him. And as everybody knows—you're a confirmed liar!"

Someone in the crowd laughed, followed by low snickering and several open catcalls. Lott flushed and his eyes went garnet with rage. His voice rose suddenly.

"You have been condemned to hang, Henry Palmer! By the Lord God Jehovah, we will not be denied!"

Palmer's smile seemed frozen. "Up until tonight, the men you've hung would have been convicted in a fair trial and duly executed. So I haven't interfered, even though you're operating outside the law. But it stops here, Wilbur! I order you—for the last time—to disband or face the consequences."

"Consequences, hell!" Lott crowed. "You can't hide behind that badge anymore!"

"Wrong again," Palmer countered. "I am the law, the *only* law! You have no authority in Virginia City."

"These men and that rope"—Lott flung his arm at the man holding the noose—"are all the authority I need!"

"Since you brought it up . . ." Palmer paused and appeared to tick off numbers. "I count only twenty men, maybe less. That wouldn't qualify as a quorum, not to mention a majority."

Lott brushed aside the objection with a broad wave. "We represent the town, the workingmen! If it's a majority you want, then we'll put it to a vote. Let the people decide!"

A ripple of approval swept through the crowd. Lott nodded and looked around with vinegary satisfaction. Then Palmer stilled the onlookers with upraised hands.

"Hear me out!" he said in a loud, commanding voice. "Where the mob rules, even innocent men fear for their lives. So I'm going to suggest a compromise that will restore order. At the same time, it will allow us to get at the truth once and for all!"

"Compromise?" Lott echoed suspiciously. "What've you got up your sleeve now?"

"Law and order!" Palmer announced in a ringing tone. "You disband your vigilantes and I'll surrender myself into the custody of Attorney General Blackthorn."

"Your political crony!" Lott hooted. "Don't make me laugh! Blackthorn's the one who put your name up for U.S. marshal. You'd walk away free as a bird!"

"On the contrary," Palmer said reasonably. "I would be charged and returned to Virginia City for trial. The issue would be settled in a court of law— by a jury of my peers."

The spectators were divided. All eyes were trained on the two men, and the miners listened raptly as their voices were pitted in counterpoint. Until now, it appeared a standoff, with neither man assured of carrying the argument. Then, abruptly, Wilbur X. Lott spread his arms and appealed directly to the crowd.

"Don't listen to him!" Lott bellowed. "He's trying to run a sandy! You let him surrender to his political pals, and he'll be long gone forever. Either we hang him tonight or we've lost. He'll escape justice—the people's justice!"

"Use your heads!" Palmer retorted. "I am a duly elected peace officer. Hang me, and the attorney general will issue a blanket murder warrant. And your name will head the list, Wilbur Lott!"

"Well, you won't be around to see it! Your term of office is about to expire . . . at the end of a rope!"

"There's the real issue here tonight!" Palmer said explosively. "You want my job! You'd crawl in bed with the devil and sell your soul for the chance to be sheriff. Say it's not so and brand yourself for the hypocrite you are!"

For a moment, Starbuck thought Palmer had won. It was a telling argument, all the more persuasive because it was true. Not a man in the crowd doubted that Wilbur X. Lott would indeed sell his soul to wear a tin star. Yet no voice was raised in Palmer's defense. Instead, a gruff buzz of murmuring broke out among the onlookers. The sound swelled and took on an ugly, guttural tone.

Lott sensed the ominous change in mood. He shook his fist in the air and cried out violently. "To the Judas Tree!"

A spate of jubilant shouts erupted from the crowd. There was a sudden milling and a mixed chorus of countermanding orders. Bloodlust transformed them on the instant into a mob.

"Get some torches!"

"No! Why take the time?"

"Do it now!"

"Where?"

"The hotel balcony!"

The miners surged off the boardwalk and engulfed Henry Palmer. He was disarmed and dragged bodily to the hotel veranda. The rope whistled over the railing of the upstairs balcony and dropped beside his head. Someone slipped the noose around his neck and cinched the knot tight. Eager hands grabbed the tail end of the rope, and the men set themselves to pull. Then Lott stayed them with a sharp command. He mounted the veranda steps and looked up at Palmer.

"Before you meet your Maker," he asked unctuously, "do you have any last words?"

"Only for you!" Palmer's eyes blazed. "I'll reserve a spot for you in hell. Don't keep me waiting too—"

"Hang him!"

The slack went out of the rope and Palmer was jerked aloft. His legs thrashed vainly at the air and his hands dug madly at the noose. His windpipe constricted and his features took on a ghastly look of terror. Then, like a thunderbolt, a gunshot split the night. A bright pearl of blood mushroomed beneath his badge and an expression of amazement crossed his face. His struggles ceased and the light in his eyes blinked out. He slumped dead.

The instant of tomblike stillness that followed was suddenly shattered. Someone yelled and pointed, and the crowd turned to look. Starbuck stood on the opposite corner, the Colt extended at shoulder level. A wisp of smoke curled out of the gun barrel, slowly drifted away. He lowered his arm.

Wilbur Lott muttered an unintelligible oath. He leaped off the veranda steps and charged across the street. The crowd parted before him, opening a corridor to the lamppost outside the café. He hauled to a stop a couple of paces from the boardwalk and grasped the lapels of his swallowtail coat. His face was ocherous.

"You've just signed your own death warrant, Mr. Detective!"

"Oh?" Starbuck's expression was sphinxlike. "How's that?"

"You killed Palmer!" Lott snarled. "You undermined the work of the Vigilance Committee!"

Starbuck gave him a dark smile. "I put a dead man out of his misery. You'll have a helluva time charging me with murder."

"I charge you with obstruction of justice!"

"Whose justice?" Starbuck laughed in his face. "Christ, you're enough to make a buzzard puke! You get your kicks watching men strangle to death, don't you?"

Lott stabbed out with a bony finger. "You'll know very shortly whether or not that's true. I impose on you the sentence of death!"

"How do you figure to make it stick?"

"Quite easily," Lott intoned. "I intend to escort you across the street and order my men to hang you. Now, hand over that gun!"

Starbuck leveled the Colt and thumbed the hammer. His voice was suddenly edged. "Why don't you take it from me?"

"Look around you," Lott said, motioning at the crowd. "Your gun won't save you from all these men! One word from me and they'll tear you to shreds."

Starbuck's eyes hooded. "One word from you and you're a dead man."

"You're bluffing!"

"Try me," Starbuck said softly. "Only take a deep breath before you do. It'll have to last a long time."

Lott seemed turned to stone. He suddenly realized a wrong word would speed him into eternity. His gaze riveted on the snout of the pistol and a vein pulsed in his forehead. A leaden moment slipped past before he glanced up at Starbuck. He swallowed nervously.

"We appear to be at a stalemate, Mr. Starbuck."

"Here's the way we'll play it, Lott. I'm leaving town tomorrow on the noon stage. You call your dogs off—give me your oath we've got a truce—and I'll let you walk away. Otherwise, your vigilante days are over."

Lott squinted at him in baffled fury. "You have my word."

"Swear it"—Starbuck wiggled the barrel of the Colt—"by your Lord God Jehovah."

"I swear it," Lott grated out. "But make sure you're on the noon stage. Our truce ends there!"

"That's the third time you've threatened my life. I generally don't allow it to happen more than once. So listen close and believe what you hear."

"A pronouncement from on high, Mr. Starbuck?"

"No, just damn good advice," Starbuck said coldly.

"Get down on your knees tonight and pray to your God that we never meet again."

"And if we do?" Lott bristled. "What then?"

Starbuck smiled. "I'll punch your ticket to the Promised Land."

"Anything more?"

"You've heard all I've got to say."

"And you have until noon tomorrow—no longer!"

Lott turned on his heel and walked away. He rejoined the vigilantes and ordered Palmer's body strung up from the hotel balcony. Then, staring straight ahead, he led his men to a nearby saloon. The crowd slowly dispersed to the dives and gaming dens along the street. Within minutes, a ghostly silence descended over the town.

Starbuck crossed to the hotel. He glanced up at the body as he mounted the stairs and entered the door. His assignment was ended in Virginia City, and nothing he'd done gave him cause for regret. Nor was he touched by remorse for Henry Palmer.

A man played the cards he was dealt.

Late the next morning Starbuck called on John Duggan. He'd had no contact with the mining association president since their initial meeting in Denver. The purpose of the call was to deliver his report, which could then be passed on to Munro Salisbury, owner of the stageline. There was also the matter of his fee.

Duggan looked like a man who had spent a sleepless night. His jowls sagged and his eyes were circled with dark rings, the lines etched deep. He greeted

Starbuck with a sallow smile and escorted him into a
cramped, utilitarian office. The room was dominated
by a scarred mahogany desk, with sectional maps of
Alder Gulch pinned to the walls and a large filing
cabinet wedged into one corner. He waved Starbuck
to a wooden armchair.

"Have a seat, Luke." He dropped into a swivel
chair behind the desk. "I had a feeling you'd be
around today."

"I'm catching the noon stage," Starbuck said, lighting a cigarette. "Figured I'd bring you up to date before I left."

"Have you read the morning newspaper?"

"No." Starbuck exhaled a cottony wad of smoke.
"A reporter tried to buttonhole me at the hotel last
night. I told him 'no comment' and gave him the fast
shuffle. What'd he write?"

Duggan unfolded a newspaper and pushed it across
the desk. "You tell me . . . fact or fiction?"

Starbuck scanned the front page, smoking quietly.
The story was emblazoned with bold headlines and
fairly simmered with purple prose. Centered on the
page was a photograph of the Judas Tree, with a limp
body dangling from a rope. His own name was prom-
inently featured throughout the text, and he found the
details surprisingly accurate. Several direct quotes
from Wilbur X. Lott were somewhat at variance with
the facts. At last, he folded the newspaper and tossed
it on the desk. He looked across at Duggan and
shrugged.

"It's pretty close to the mark. They're a little confused about the Carver girl and how I tracked down

Skinner. But there's not a whole lot I'd add. Probably couldn't have written a better report myself."

"How do you think the reporter found out we hired you?"

"Beats me," Starbuck admitted. "I guess that's why they're called newshounds. What makes you ask?"

"Wilbur Lott," Duggan said, tapping the newspaper. "You'll note he's trying to take a major share of the credit. We feel that's not in our best interests."

"When you say 'our,' I take it you mean the mining association?"

"I do indeed," Duggan acknowledged. "We hired you—along with the stage company—and we want the credit. Lott had no part in breaking the case!"

"Call a news conference," Starbuck suggested. "Let the facts speak for themselves."

"Would you agree to a joint interview?"

"Nope," Starbuck said shortly. "I try to steer clear of reporters. You don't need me, anyway. All you have to do is point out one simple fact. Lott hasn't done anything but hang a bunch of people."

"Unfortunately, he'll claim otherwise, and the public has a tendency to believe what it reads in print."

Duggan launched into a long-winded dissertation on the politics of Virginia City. Starbuck listened with only half an ear. He subscribed to no particular ideology and he'd always considered politics a dirty word. To him, it was a matter of supreme indifference which faction controlled the political apparatus. By whatever name, the party in power was no less corrupt than its opponents. He stubbed out his cigarette as the civics lesson drew to a close. Duggan concluded by once more asking him to submit to a newspaper interview.

"Sorry," Starbuck replied with a poker face. "You hired me to kill a gang leader. By my count, you got your money's worth several times over. Let's just leave it there."

Duggan studied him with a reproachful frown. "Doesn't it bother you that Lott might end up running Virginia City?"

"I'm not my brother's keeper." Starbuck cracked a smile. "It's a job better suited to preachers and politicians."

"Suppose I told you Lott and his vigilantes hanged an innocent man this morning?"

"Anyone I know?"

"His name was Jack Slade."

"Are you saying he had nothing to do with the robbers?"

"Nothing whatsoever!" Duggan looked worried. "He was a saloon tough and a general troublemaker."

"Why'd Lott hang him?"

"Slade picked a fight with one of the vigilantes last night. Lott ordered him out of town by sunup and he refused to leave. So now he's decorating the Judas Tree."

Starbuck's jawline hardened. "I reckon that means it's started."

"What's started?" The worry lines on Duggan's forehead deepened. "I don't follow you."

"Sooner or later vigilantes get around to hanging all the badmen and desperados. But it's a goddamn hard habit to break! So some unlucky stiff winds up being lynched before things get back to normal. With Lott, that might take a while . . . and a few more unlucky stiffs."

"Now that you mention it," Duggan said uneasily, "I understand Lott threatened to string you up."

"Yeah, he had some such notion."

"Then all the more reason to grant the press an interview. You could do Virginia City a favor and settle a personal score—all in one stroke!"

Starbuck deliberated a moment. "I reckon not. One way or another, the grave always straightens out hunchbacks."

"Hunchbacks?" Duggan stared at him. "What's that got to do with Lott?"

A slow smile spread across Starbuck's face. "It's an old saying. Some men spend their lives trying to get themselves killed. Wilbur Lott fits the mold."

Duggan hesitated, considering. "I also heard you threatened to kill him."

"Nooo," Starbuck said slowly. "It was more on the order of a promise."

"Hmmm." Duggan eyed him with a scrutinizing look. "You wouldn't have a crystal ball, would you, Luke?"

"I'm a detective, not a swami."

"Sometimes there's only a fine line separating promise and prophecy."

"Let's just say"—Starbuck smiled cryptically—"Wilbur Lott's a hunchback with one foot in the grave."

"Hallelujah!" Duggan laughed. "I've got an idea

Virginia City will be in your debt for a long time to come."

"That reminds me," Starbuck said without expression. "Our deal was half down and half on delivery. I delivered last night."

Still chortling, Duggan opened his desk drawer and pulled out a signed check. "Like I said, I thought you might drop around today. I believe the balance due was five thousand."

"On the nose." Starbuck inspected the check and tucked it into his shirt pocket. "Much obliged."

"Quite the contrary," Duggan said gratefully. "We're the ones who are obligated. You did a whiz-bang of a job, Luke."

"All in a day's work."

"Amen to that!"

Duggan walked him to the door. There he thrust out his hand and warmly pumped Starbuck's arm. With a wave, Starbuck stepped outside and strolled off in the direction of the hotel. He was whistling tunelessly under his breath.

Some while later Starbuck emerged from the stage-line office. He handed the driver his ticket and waited until his warbag was stowed securely in the luggage boot. Then he climbed aboard the coach and took a window seat. On impulse, he fished out his pocket watch and checked the time. He saw it was twelve-o-nine, and his eyes immediately swept the street. Wilbur Lott and the vigilantes were nowhere in sight.

The twelve o'clock deadline had come and gone.

Yet Lott had apparently weighed the wisdom of revoking their truce. Starbuck thought it a damn shame.

High noon seemed an appropriate death hour . . . for a hunchback.

Chapter Seventeen

The Alcazar Variety Theater was mobbed. Scarcely a table remained vacant, and the barroom was crowded to capacity. With the first show still a half hour away, it was already standing room only. Lola Montana, as usual, would play to a packed house.

Jack Brady, proprietor of the Alcazar, stood near the door. His thumbs were hooked in his vest and a cigar jutted from his mouth like a burnt tusk. The turnout seldom failed to put him in an expansive mood, and tonight he looked enormously pleased with himself. The star of his show was the toast of the town, the single greatest drawing card in Denver. Only today he'd boosted her salary to a level that none of his competitors would dare match. He was congratulating himself on his foresight when a commotion at the door attracted his attention.

Starbuck was trapped just inside the entranceway. Voices were raised in congratulations and well-wishers ganged around for a quick handshake. Brady and a couple of bouncers rescued him from the crowd. The housemen charged into the melee and roughly cleared the well-wishers away. Then, their arms spread wide, they formed a protective cordon. The theater owner greeted Starbuck with an ebullient grin.

"Welcome back, Luke!"

"Thanks," Starbuck mumbled, eyeing the crowd. "I feel like I just stepped into a goldfish bowl."

"The price of fame!" Brady laughed. "You'd better get used to it."

"I'd sooner have a little privacy."

"No more!" Brady crowed. "That's a thing of the past, Luke. You're a public figure now!"

"Who says?"

"Everybody and his brother!" Brady said gleefully. "Don't you read the papers?"

"Not lately," Starbuck grouched. "I've been on a train for the last couple of days."

Starbuck had pulled into town earlier that evening. He'd gone directly to his hotel suite, where he treated himself to a long soak in a hot bath. Afterward, he had ordered supper from room service and penned two messages to be delivered by a bellboy. One went to Lola, and the other went to Horace Griffin, division superintendent of Wells Fargo. Then he'd dressed and caught a hansom cab to the Alcazar. He hadn't read a newspaper since departing Virginia City.

"Take my word for it!" Brady assured him. "Half the goddamn world knows who you are tonight. You're big news—headline news!"

"Worse luck," Starbuck said with a pained expression. "Got a table for me, Jack?"

"The best in the house—reserved and waiting!"

The bouncers led the way. A path opened before them, and Brady escorted him to a table near the orchestra pit. Starbuck felt somewhat like a clown in a parade. All eyes were on him and a buzz of excitement swept through the theater. He was no sooner seated than a waiter appeared with a bucket of iced champagne. Brady fussed around longer than necessary, clearly delighted with the sideshow atmosphere. Finally, Starbuck was alone at the table. He lit a cigarette and tried to ignore the stares.

A short while later Horace Griffin arrived. Brady again made a production of escorting the Wells Fargo superintendent to the table. Griffin seemed amused by the attention and put on a show of wringing Starbuck's hand. The waiter materialized with another glass and deftly poured champagne. Then, at last, the activity around the table slacked off.

"Happy days!" Griffin hoisted his glass in a toast. "Looks like you're the man of the hour, Luke."

"Don't rub it in," Starbuck said gruffly. "Jack Brady already beat the drum till my ears are ringing."

"I thought it was a celebration! Isn't that why you invited me to join you?"

"Not exactly," Starbuck informed him. "We've still got some unfinished business."

"What sort of business?"

"How would you like to recover part of the stolen gold?"

"From the Virginia City holdups?"

"That's the idea."

Griffin was openly surprised. "I'd like that a lot, Luke. Needless to say, it would be a feather in both our caps. The home office might even come through with a bonus."

Starbuck grinned. "I never turn down money."

"What's involved in recovering the gold?"

"A lawyer and a shovel."

"I beg your pardon?"

Starbuck pulled a small ledger from his pocket. He briefly explained that the ledger itemized Cyrus Skinner's gold deposits in a Salt Lake City bank. He suggested that Wells Fargo institute a court suit—with the ledger as prima facie evidence—against Skinner's estate. Then he produced a piece of paper, with a hand-drawn diagram of the Virginia City livery stable. He recounted the story of the stagecoach robbery—in league with Frank Yeager and the gang—and how he'd later hidden his share of the loot. A bold X on the diagram marked the correct stall. He told Griffin the gold was buried a foot or so down, not counting manure. A shovel and a few minutes' digging would do the trick.

"With Skinner's estate," he concluded, "and what you find in the stall, it'll nudge a hundred and ten thousand dollars. Not exactly what you'd call chicken feed."

"How true!" Griffin took a thoughtful sip of champagne. "I can't help but wonder about the others . . . Yeager and Stimson and Henry Palmer."

"What about them?"

"Well, it's possible their share of the robberies might be recovered. Would you be interested in looking into it—for a percentage?"

Starbuck wagged his head back and forth. "I was hired to get them . . . not their bankrolls."

"You're perfectly right!" Griffin agreed quickly. "We'll put a lawyer to work on it."

"Have him contact me," Starbuck offered. "I could point him in the right direction."

"I will indeed!" Griffin once more lifted his glass. "Here's to you! Wells Fargo won't forget the job you've done."

Starbuck's grin widened. "I'll depend on it, Horace."

"Good evening, Luke!"

Ned Buntline approached the table. He halted with a fraudulent smile and an outstretched hand. Starbuck studiously declined the handshake. He looked the writer up and down.

"Where'd you drop from, Buntline?"

"New York," Buntline replied, lowering his arm. "I came in on the evening train."

"What brings you to Denver?"

"You do!" Buntline gave Griffin a perfuntory nod and seated himself. "I'm here to make you a millionaire, Luke!"

Starbuck regarded him with impassive curiosity. "I thought we already had this discussion."

"That was before!"

"Before what?"

"Before Virginia City!" Buntline said with cheery vigor. "Before you routed a gang of robbers and singlehandedly faced down a vigilante mob!"

"How'd you hear about that?"

"You're too modest!" Buntline's smirk turned to a smug grin. "The newspapers have all but made your name a household word. You're a sensation back east!"

"So?"

"So you're famous!" Buntline cackled. "You killed five men—including a renegade sheriff—all in a matter of weeks!"

Starbuck looked annoyed. "I shot Palmer the way you would a crippled horse. I don't take any pride in it."

"A trifle!" Buntline said confidently. "Only one point has significance. You are the foremost lawman on the western frontier!"

"I'm not a lawman," Starbuck corrected him. "I'm a private detective."

"Whatever you are"—Buntline's eyes took on a tinsel glitter—"you're the deadliest mankiller extant. You've overshadowed Wild Bill Hickok and Wes Hardin and all the others. You stand alone at the apex of your profession!"

Starbuck's eyebrows drew together in a frown. "I don't travel in the company of gunmen. I told you once and I'll tell you again—I'm a detective."

Buntline appraised him with a crafty look. "By any name, you've captured the public's imagination. Virginia City was an epic struggle—good versus evil—and you're now something more than a nameless man-hunter. You are on the verge of greatness!"

"Forget it," Starbuck said shortly. "Go peddle your snake oil somewhere else."

"Confound it, Luke!" Buntline objected. "Listen to reason! You'll make a fortune off of dime novels and stage appearances. Within a year, you'll be rich as Midas!"

Starbuck hesitated just long enough to lend emphasis to his words. "Get the wax out of your ears and pay real close attention. I don't want any part of you or your schemes—and that's final!"

"Stop and think!" Buntline persisted. "It's not just the money we're talking about! I'm offering you something few men ever attain. Sign with me, and I'll make you part of our mythology . . . *one of the immortals!*"

"You've overstayed your welcome." Starbuck jerked a thumb toward the street. "Hit the bricks, and be damn quick about it!"

"You're passing up the opportunity of—"

Starbuck stood and moved swiftly around the table. He snatched Buntline out of his chair and spun him around. One hand took hold of the writer's coat collar and the other grabbed him by the seat of his pants. Then Starbuck danced him up on tiptoe and marched off at a fast clip.

"Gangway! We're comin' through!"

The crowd split as though cleaved apart. Starbuck hustled Buntline out of the theater and through the barroom. One of the housemen obligingly opened the door and stepped aside. Halting at the last moment, Starbuck lifted the writer bodily and gave him the bum's rush. Buntline landed on his rump and bounced across the sidewalk. His hat went flying and he rolled face down in the gutter.

Grinning broadly, Starbuck dusted his hands and walked back to the theater. All around him men cheered and applauded and pressed forward to slap him on the shoulder. As he approached his table the orchestra thumped to life and the curtain swished open. A chorus line, led by Lola Montana, cavorted out of the wings. Their legs flashed and they bounded onstage in a swirl of skirts. Then the tempo of the music quickened and they went into a high-stepping dance routine.

Lola stared past the footlights and her eyes fastened on him. She pranced downstage, her bloomers revealed in a showy cakewalk, and gave him a dazzling smile. The chorus girls squealed and kicked higher, and Lola dimpled her lips in a beestung pucker. Her hand touched her mouth and she blew him a kiss.

Starbuck sat down to a thunderous ovation.

Late that night, Starbuck unlocked the door to his hotel suite. Lola preceded him through the foyer and tossed her cape on a chair. Then she turned and stepped into his arms. She kissed him long and passionately.

"Ummm!" She groaned and lightly caressed his cheek. "That's sweeter than sugar and twice as nice!"

"Careful what you wish for," Starbuck joked, tightening his embrace. "It's liable to come true."

"Not so fast!" Lola slipped from his arms. "I want to change into something more comfortable, and I want a drink." She lowered one eyelid in a bawdy wink. "Then I want you—all night!"

Starbuck watched her disappear into the bedroom. He chuckled, amused by her antics, and crossed to the liquor cabinet. There, he collected a couple of glasses and a brandy decanter, and moved to the sofa. After placing everything on the coffee table, he shrugged out of his suit jacket and loosened his tie. He filled both glasses and left them standing. Then he lounged back on the sofa and lit a cigarette.

A time passed before Lola returned. She wore a sheer cambric peignoir and high-heeled slippers. Her breasts were visible through the gauzy fabric, and a bare leg showed as she crossed the room. She smelled faintly of lilac.

Starbuck extinguished his cigarette. She sat down beside him, and he handed her a snifter of brandy. Without a word, they clinked glasses and sipped. Their eyes met and held, and something unspoken passed between them. She ran her tongue over her lips and smiled.

"Welcome home, lover."

"I'll second the motion."

"Did you miss me?"

"What do you think?"

"I think maybe you did . . . a little bit."

"Now you're fishing for compliments."

"Well, a girl does like to hear sweet talk!"

"Talk's cheap." Starbuck nodded to a jewel box on the coffee table. "How about something more permanent?"

"A present!" Lola's eyes got big and round. "For me?"

"Open it and see."

The jewel box was large and wide, covered with plush velvet. Lola opened it slowly and then suddenly caught her breath in a sharp gasp. Inside was a diamond and sapphire pendant, mounted on a necklace of interlocked diamond rosettes. The stones sparkled richly in the lamplight, and she seemed mesmerized by the interplay of colors. Then she snapped the lid closed and clutched the box to her breast. Her eyes filled with tears.

"Oh, Luke!" She blinked, and a teardrop rolled down her cheek. "It's beautiful!"

"Hell, don't cry!" Starbuck's grin was so wide it was almost a laugh. "You're supposed to be happy!"

"You dope!" Lola sniffed and clutched the box tighter. "Why do you think I'm crying?"

"Yeah—" Starbuck looked embarrassed. "I just never saw you cry before, that's all."

"Some presents are worth crying over! God, it must have cost a fortune, Luke!"

"Only a small fortune," Starbuck said with a waggish grin. "I wanted you to have a memento of Virginia City. I couldn't have done it without you."

"Honestly?" Lola wiped the tears away. "You're not just saying that?"

"Cross my heart." Starbuck stitched a cross over his shirt pocket. "Without you, I would've never got wind of Alice Carver. And without her, I'd have never broken the case. So I owe it all to you."

Lola took another quick peek at the pendant. Then her eyes cleared and she fixed him with a sly look. "You're a terrible liar, Luke Starbuck."

"I wouldn't lie about a thing like that!"

"Yes, you would!" Lola's laugh was low and infectious. "You paid more for this pendant than you earned on the case. How do you explain that?"

"Nothing simpler." Starbuck gave her a jolly wink. "You were due a present long before Virginia City."

"Why?" Lola asked, a devilish glint in her eye. "I want to hear you tell me."

A smile tugged at the corner of Starbuck's mouth. "I reckon I just did."

Lola knew better than to push him too far. In his own way, he had indeed told her what she wanted to hear. He was an emotional nomad; therefore, his choice of words was always oblique. Yet, however roundabout, it was enough for Lola. She adroitly switched to another topic.

"How long will I have the pleasure of your company?"

"How long you figure you could stand me?"

"Don't play cat and mouse!" Lola shook a rougish finger at him. "You checked your mail before you came to the theater—didn't you?"

"So what?"

"So tell me!" Lola mocked his grumpy expression. "How long until your next case?"

"Whoa, now!" Starbuck protested. "Don't get any harebrained ideas!"

"Why, whatever are you talking about?"

"You know damn well!" Starbuck said sternly. "You got a taste of undercover work and you like it. Just don't expect to tag along on every case!"

Lola let the remark pass. "Something in your mail must have been very interesting!"

"Goddamn, aren't a man's secrets safe anymore?"

"Not from me," Lola cooed, batting her lashes. "You're an open book, lover!"

Starbuck sat there with a funny look in his eye. After a moment he chuckled softly. "A fellow from

Santa Fe wants to see me. His letter sounded the least bit urgent."

"Outlaws in Santa Fe?"

"High-class outlaws," Starbuck confided. "I got the impression he wants to talk about the Santa Fe Ring."

"Omigawd!" Lola yelped. "Weren't they the ones behind the Lincoln County war?"

"Nobody's proved it . . . yet."

"When would you leave?"

"All depends," Starbuck said with a shrug. "I wired the fellow and told him to hop the next train to Denver."

"In that case, we shouldn't waste any time."

"What'd you have in mind?"

"Something naughty and wild!"

"Got any samples?"

Lola laughed a sultry, deep-throated laugh. She scooted across the sofa and snuggled close. Her arms went around his neck and she pulled his head down. Then she kissed him with fierce abandon, her tongue darting his mouth. When at last they separated, her voice was warm and husky.

"Ooo how I want you! Take me to bed, lover!"

Starbuck took her.

Epilogue

El Paso
September 22, 1883

Starbuck stepped onto the veranda of the Parker House Hotel. Beyond the mountains, the last rays of sunset streaked the sky like dull fire. A bluish dusk slowly settled over El Paso.

The hotel was situated on the east side of San Jacinto Plaza. From the veranda Starbuck had a commanding view of the broad square and the uptown business district. He walked forward and took a seat in a cane-bottomed rocker. He lit a cigarette and loosened the Colt in its crossdraw holster. Then he set the rocker into motion.

A patient hunter, Starbuck let his mind wander while he waited. He recalled hearing that the conquistadores had originally named the town El Paso del Norte. Surrounded by mountains, it lay nestled in the Tularosa Basin and provided a natural pass to the north over the Franklin range. To the southwest, across the Rio Grande, lay the Sierra Madre range. The mountains formed a backdrop for El Paso's counterpart on the Mexican shoreline, Paso del Norte. Yesterday, on the train, he'd heard that Paso del Norte was a place where gringo lawmen seldom ventured. He thought it a revealing comment, all part and parcel of a widely accepted belief. El Paso itself was considered the toughest border town on the frontier.

Formerly a wilderness crossroads, El Paso had been little more than a stopover to somewhere else. The trail from Sante Fe to Mexico City ran directly through the plaza, while the stage route connecting San Antonio with the Pacific Coast meandered off in the opposite direction. Only two years ago, with the arrival of the Southern Pacific Railroad, the sleepy village had undergone a startling transformation. The daily trains from east Texas had disgorged a horde of saloon-keepers and cardsharps, whores and gunmen, and the usual assortment of hardcases. There were fortunes to be made in a boomtime bordertown, and El Paso welcomed harlot and outlaw alike with open arms. The town mushroomed under an uneasy alliance of commerce and vice.

The danger to lawmen was in no way exaggerated. El Paso's first marshal had lasted only a few months. His replacement, a former Texas Ranger, was Dallas Stoudenmire. Within a week of taking office, Stoudenmire had killed three men and established himself as a fighting marshal. Only last year, after running afoul of the sporting crowd, Stoudenmire had been removed from office. Some months later he'd been killed in a shootout with the Manning brothers, who allegedly controlled much of the vice district. The message was clear to men who wore a badge. El Paso was an open town, with no great pretense of law and order. A peace officer who believed otherwise risked his life on a daily basis.

Staring out across the plaza, Starbuck thought it a point worth remembering. He had arrived by train only last night, and he was under no illusions about his own safety. In the event he was recognized, there were any number of men in El Paso who would gladly gun him down from behind. Not the least among them was the man he sought. Still, he had opted to work openly rather than operate undercover. He'd come here to kill Wilbur X. Lott.

Hardly to his surprise, Starbuck's prediction regarding the Virginia City vigilantes had proved correct. Some six weeks past, Lott and his band of stranglers had lynched a man mistakenly identified as a horse thief. Lott, who had failed in his bid for political office, was already at odds with the authorities. The hanging of yet another innocent man merely quickened his downfall. He was charged with murder and promptly fled Virginia City. A fugitive warrant was issued and the territorial governor posted a reward of a thousand dollars. He was wanted dead or alive.

The reward was a matter of no consequence to Starbuck. He had a personal score to settle, and the law had provided the legal means. While he couldn't spare the time for an investigation, he had no intention of allowing Lott to escape justice. After reflecting on it, he'd decided to approach the problem in a roundabout manner. Through Jack Murphy, his chief informant in the Denver underworld, he had put out feelers across the West. Among thieves and desperados, the moccasin telegraph was the principal source of information. Over a month passed before word drifted back to Starbuck via the grapevine. Wilbur X. Lott was holed up in Paso del Norte.

According to Starbuck's informant, Lott spent most of his time on the Mexican side of the Rio Grande. Paso del Norte was a sanctuary for gringo badmen, immune to the laws of extradition and the long arm of American peace officers. Lott lived across the border and apparently visited El Paso only after dark. He was known to prefer the company of gringa women, and his favorite hangout was the White Elephant Saloon, on the west side of the plaza. He was operating under the alias William Latham, and these days he sported a beard. He had no known associates in El Paso.

Last night, upon arriving in town, Starbuck had checked into the hotel. Except for meals, he'd kept to his room throughout the day. His plan was simple and direct. He would stay out of sight during the day and thereby avoid the risk of alerting Lott. At sundown, he would take up a post on the hotel veranda and maintain a watch on the White Elephant. Sooner or later, his quarry would show. Then he would walk across the plaza and perform the job by the most expedient means. Tonight's stakeout was the first of what might very well prove to be a marathon. Yet, however long it took, he had no qualms or reservations. He was prepared to wait for the chance to kill Wilbur Lott.

Starbuck's vigil paid off on his third cigarette. He

saw Lott appear from Main Street, which angled off in the direction of the bridge connecting El Paso with Paso del Norte. The streetlamps were lighted and the former vigilante was easily recognizable. The beard he'd grown had altered his appearance, but his cadaverous frame and hooklike nose were impossible to disguise. He crossed to the west side of the plaza with the air of a man whose troubles are few and far behind. A moment later he disappeared through the doors of the White Elephant.

No great believer in luck, Starbuck nonetheless took it as a good omen. To locate Lott on the first night seemed at the very least providential. He stood and ground his cigarette underfoot. Tugging his suit jacket over the Colt, he moved directly to the veranda stairs. The prospect of killing a man worked on him like some mystical anodyne. At such times, his heartbeat slowed, and his nerves, as though cauterized, simply ceased to function. He operated solely on instinct and reflex, some atavistic sense tuned not so much to survival as the need to kill swiftly. He crossed the plaza with no thought of personal danger. His whole attitude was zeroed on the task ahead.

The White Elephant was a cut above most bordertown watering holes. A long mahogany bar dominated one side of the room. Behind the counter a massive French mirror, flanked by nude paintings, adorned the wall. Opposite the bar was a row of gaming tables, and toward the rear of the room was a small dance floor. A piano player and a fiddler provided the entertainment, while a bevy of saloon girls ministered to those with a taste for companionship. The crowd was boisterous and loud, the atmosphere congenial. No one paid Starbuck the slightest attention.

Wilbur Lott stood with his elbows hooked over the bar and one foot firmly planted on the brass rail. He had a drink in one hand and a bosomy redhead attached to his arm. His mode of dress was still somewhat funereal, with a swallowtail coat topped off by a broad-brimmed hat. Beneath the coat, a bulge on his right hip betrayed the presence of a holstered pistol. His expression was that of a man with lechery on his mind. He looked as if he were swapping dirty ideas with the redhead.

Starbuck wedged in beside him. Lott's concentration was on the girl, and several moments passed without incident. Then, after a wayward glance in the backbar mirror, Lott suddenly stiffened. His eyes went wide with fright and he pushed off the counter. Starbuck nodded with a wry grin.

"How's tricks, Wilbur?"

"I—" Lott faltered, his face ashen. "What do you want?"

"Dumb question," Starbuck needled him. "You're a fugitive from justice."

"You have no authority in Texas!"

"Why stand on formalities?" Starbuck quipped. "Kiss your lady friend goodbye and we'll be on our way."

Lott glowered at him through slitted eyes. "I'm not going anywhere with you!"

"Yeah, you are," Starbuck said evenly. "Way it works out, you've got a choice. Come along peaceable, and I'll take you back to Montana. Otherwise, you and the undertaker are set for a one-way ride."

"No!" Lott said with sudden resolve. "I won't fight and you won't kill me in cold blood!"

"Wanna bet?" Starbuck let go a ferocious laugh. "The reward dodger says dead or alive. Open season on Wilbur X. Lott."

The redhead believed him. She gently disengaged her hand from Lott's arm and eased away from the bar. For all his bravado, Lott too sensed his life was in imminent peril. He saw in Starbuck's gaze a look of predatory eagerness. His attitude underwent an abrupt turnaround.

"Listen to me, Starbuck!" His voice was heavy, stark. "I grant you we hung the wrong man. But we didn't know that at the time. It was a mistake—an accident!"

"How do you accidentally lynch somebody?"

"He was on a stolen horse! We didn't find out till later he'd bought it off the real thief. By then, it was too late!"

"Pretty flimsy," Starbuck said with a sardonic look. "The law don't issue a dead-or-alive warrant on accidental homicide. Sounds like you hung one too many men, Wilbur."

"It wasn't that!" Lott muttered vehemently. "I made too many political enemies, and they were out to get me. Any excuse would've done!"

"Tit for tat," Starbuck observed. "You hung a whole slew of men over nothing but politics. Why shouldn't somebody hang you for the same reason?"

"For God's sake!" Lott implored. "It was an accident—I swear it!"

"Tell you what," Starbuck said in a musing tone. "I never was one to cause a man undue suffering. So I'll give you the same break I gave Henry Palmer."

"Palmer!" Lott blanched. "You shot him!"

"Square through the heart," Starbuck nodded sagely. "Quick and painless, and it don't spoil the looks of the corpse."

Sweat popped out on Lott's forehead. "I don't care much for that idea."

"Well, like I told you," Starbuck said matter-of-factly. "You've got a choice between me and Montana. Course, if I was you, I wouldn't let nobody strangle me to death. That's a goddamn hard way to cash out."

A vivid image of the Judas Tree flashed through Lott's mind. His throat constricted and his face turned pasty white. "I guess I'll have to chance it."

"Suit yourself."

Starbuck deliberately turned his head sideways. He signaled the barkeep, seemingly unconcerned about Lott. Yet, alert to any movement, he watched the large mirror out of the corner of his eye. The barkeep bustled forward.

"Yessir!"

"Who's your town marshal?"

"Jim Gillett!"

"Send somebody to fetch him—on the double!"

"What's the problem?"

"Get him over here and you'll find out."

Lott listened to the exchange with mounting dread. His expression became immobile and dark, and the muscles in his jaw knotted. Then, suddenly, he decided to risk it all on one play. His eyes flashed with a formidable glitter and his arm swept the swallowtail coat aside. His hand closed over the butt of his pistol.

Starbuck seemed to move not at all. The Colt appeared out of nowhere and in the same instant his head swiveled around. Lott's eyes were marblelike with shock, and he somehow looked betrayed. As his pistol cleared leather Starbuck feathered the trigger and the Colt belched flame. Lott stood perfectly still, a great splotch of red covering his breastbone. Then the pistol slipped from his fingers and his legs buckled. He slowly slumped to the floor.

Holstering the Colt, Starbuck knelt beside the fallen man. Lott lay with his head propped up against the brass rail, his hat tilted askew. A trickle of blood seeped out of the corner of his mouth and his breathing was ragged. He stared at Starbuck with a glassy expression.

"You tricked me."

"You tricked yourself, Wilbur."

"Dirty . . . pool . . ."

The words ended in a gurgled cough and Lott's eyes rolled back in his head. Starbuck studied the face a moment, almost a clinical examination. Then he leaned forward and closed the eyelids with his fingertips. He stood and nodded to the barkeep.

"Tell the marshal he'll find me over at the hotel."

"Yessir, cap'n! I shorely will!"

Outside, Starbuck crossed the plaza at a measured stride. He heard again the last words of Wilbur X. Lott. The thought occurred that what he'd done was indeed dirty pool. But, then, there were no rules on

the killing ground. He smiled, not in the least troubled
he'd sent a strangler to the grave. In the end, for those
who held themselves above the law, only one code
prevailed.

Some men deserved to die.